"Did you expect me to sleep in here with you?"

"We should talk about that." Cash felt Presley stiffen in his arms. "I want you here, Pres. In this bed. But we should be clear about what this is...and what it's not."

"You mean you aren't going to marry me and make an honest woman out of me after that?"

Cash's face broadcasted myriad emotions.

"God, your face! I'm kidding. Cash, honestly."

He gave her an unsure half smile. "I knew that."

"I'm not the girl you left at Florida State. I grew up, too, you know. I learned how the world worked."

She wasn't so foolish to believe that sex had the power to change the past. The past was him promising to wait for her and then leaving.

This was the present, and she knew how it worked.

"I had a great time," she continued with a grin. "I'm looking forward to doing it again if you're up to the task."

* * *

Second Chance Love Song by Jessica Lemmon is part of the Dynasties: Beaumont Bay series.

Recycling programs
for this product may
not exist in your area.

ISBN-13: 978-1-335-23289-2

Second Chance Love Song

Copyright © 2021 by Jessica Lemmon

This edition published by arrangement with Harlequin Books S.A.

For questions and comments about the quality of this book,
please contact us at CustomerService@Harlequin.com.

Harlequin Enterprises ULC
22 Adelaide St. West, 40th Floor
Toronto, Ontario M5H 4E3, Canada
www.Harlequin.com

Printed in U.S.A.

DYNASTIES

Where family loyalties and passions collide.

Harlequin Desire brings you Dynasties—delicious, dramatic miniseries that span generations, include an engaging cast of characters and sweep you into the world of the American elite. From luxury ranch retreats to the stages of Nashville, from the sagas of powerful families to the redeeming power of passion... don't miss a single installment of Dynasties!

Dynasties: Beaumont Bay

What happens in Beaumont Bay stays in Beaumont Bay. This is the bedroom community where Nashville comes to play!

Twin Games in Music City by Jules Bennett
—available now
Second Chance Love Song by Jessica Lemmon
—available now
Fake Engagement, Nashville Style by Jules Bennett
—available June 2021
Good Twin Gone Country by Jessica Lemmon
—available July 2021

Dynasties: The Carey Center

The Carey family works hard and plays harder as they build a performance space to rival Carnegie Hall!
From *USA TODAY* bestselling author Maureen Child
Available September, October, November and December 2021

Dynasties: The Ryders

For this perfect all-American family,
image is everything. Until a DNA ancestry test
reveals secrets they've hidden for generations...
From Joss Wood
Available February, March, April and May 2022

Dynasties: The Eddington Heirs

In Point du Sable, this empire is under siege.
Only family unity and the power of love can save it!
From Zuri Day
Available July, August, September and October 2022

Dear Reader,

I love a heartbreaking love song. One where the singer shares his sad loss and still hasn't quite recovered from it. In Cash Sutherland's case, that heartbreaking love song made him an award-winning superstar. Now he's doomed to perform "Lightning" over and over, reliving his biggest regret under the bright lights of a lonely stage.

For Presley Cole, "Lightning" is her chance to uncover the best-kept secret in country music and write what could be the juiciest story of her career. Her task? Go to Beaumont Bay and sweet-talk Cash into confessing who he wrote this song about.

I probably don't have to tell you that Cash isn't receptive to talking about his past heartbreak—especially with Presley, the girl whose heart he so thoroughly broke in college. But she isn't dissuaded. During her stay in the Bay, she's determined to find out the truth before leaving him behind the way he left her ten years ago.

I hope you enjoy the second installment of Dynasties: Beaumont Bay, and I also hope you'll check out the rest of the series, which has been a delightful collaboration with *USA TODAY* bestselling author Jules Bennett. We had so much fun writing it for you!

Happy reading,

Jessica Lemmon

www.JessicaLemmon.com

JESSICA LEMMON

———

SECOND CHANCE LOVE SONG

A former job-hopper, **Jessica Lemmon** resides in Ohio with her husband and rescue dog. She holds a degree in graphic design, which is currently gathering dust in an impressive frame. When she's not writing supersexy heroes, she can be found cooking, drawing, drinking coffee (okay, wine) and eating potato chips. She firmly believes God gifts us with talents for a purpose, and with His help, you can create the life you want.

Jessica is a social media junkie who loves to hear from readers. You can learn more at jessicalemmon.com.

Books by Jessica Lemmon

Harlequin Desire

Dallas Billionaires Club

Lone Star Lovers
A Snowbound Scandal
A Christmas Proposition

Kiss and Tell

His Forbidden Kiss
One Wild Kiss
One Last Kiss

Dynasties: Beaumont Bay

Second Chance Love Song

Visit her Author Profile page at Harlequin.com, or jessicalemmon.com, for more titles.

You can also find Jessica Lemmon on Facebook, along with other Harlequin Desire authors, at Facebook.com/harlequindesireauthors!

Prologue

10 years ago
Florida State University

Sparks sizzled along Presley Cole's skin with each stinging raindrop falling from the sky. She felt as if she might go up in smoke—or up in steam, given they'd been caught in the downpour.

She could hardly believe she was standing outside her dormitory building making out with Cash Sutherland. *The* Cash Sutherland who, by some miracle, had essentially become her boyfriend.

Sure, they'd been out a few times—to dinners or parties—but she'd counted herself lucky to simply be in his presence. She'd never dreamed he'd stick around for innocent nights ending with them still wearing their clothes. Not when there were so many other beautiful girls at this school who would gladly sleep with him.

Especially when Presley had let him know she wouldn't. Oh, she wanted to, but her feelings for him were too big, too frightening, to wrap her head around. She was scared they would overtake her and drag her down, especially if she crossed that boundary. And then, if the worst happened and he left her, how would she recover?

You're worth the wait.

He'd told her so last night, after delivering a hand-in-her-pants orgasm that rivaled any in her limited sexual past. She'd apologized for not going further, for making him wait, for leaving him hanging. He'd pulled her into his arms and kissed her some more, the sturdy ridge of his erection pressing the side of her leg, and told her to stop worrying about him.

Seriously, he was too good to be true.

He pulled his lips from hers and smoothed her wet hair away from her face. They were leaning against the brick wall, the overhang not doing much to keep them dry. Not with the wind blowing the way it was. Hurricane season was upon them.

Her eyes caught the splint bracing his middle and ring fingers. She tipped her head back to admire his soulful dark eyes and sharp nose, his full mouth that usually smiled at her. He hadn't smiled much lately. As if the injury had stolen his joy.

"Does your finger hurt?" she asked. He'd broken it on the field, which put him temporarily out of the game. Not good for a senior who could be scouted by the NFL any day now. And yet his biggest complaint was that he couldn't play guitar while wearing a splint. His passion for singing and songwriting had blown her "hot jock" theory out of the water the first time she'd spoken to him. She'd thought she had him figured out, but he surprised her at every turn. The gorgeous guy who played a grueling, demanding sport quite well was also capable of singing tender lyrics with the rawest emotion. No wonder she was crazy about him.

"Pres, I have to tell you something."

That statement was delivered in an even monotone, so she lied and told herself he wasn't about to share bad news. But, somehow, her body knew. Her arms began to shake and her teeth chattered like she was standing in a blizzard instead of a Florida rainstorm.

"Do you want to come up?" she asked, hoping to delay whatever damning news might come. "It's pretty wet out here."

His mouth hitched to one side, not quite returning her nervous smile. Then he took a deep breath, one that expanded his chest and lifted his shoulders. It was late, it was dark. They'd spent all day in class and then most of the evening studying at the library. She was tired and so was he. Maybe that's what this was about, she lied to herself some more.

"Come up." She grasped his uninjured hand. "I'll heat some cocoa and we can curl up on my bed and talk." She pushed to her tiptoes, planted a soft kiss on the side of his mouth and then whispered, "Or not talk."

He looked like he might say no but nodded instead. She took it as a win as he walked with her up the stairs, as they entered her dorm room, as she traded her wet T-shirt for a dry one. But when she pulled him toward the bed for a make-out session, his stormy mood returned, and with it came her teeth-chattering worry. Something was definitely wrong.

Moments later she found out what.

He'd broken up with her that night, leaving her crying on her bed. The storm outside grew more intense, but it had nothing on the one inside her. Lightning flashed, and she watched out the window through puffy, gritty eyes. Thunder raged, the sound drowning out the sound of her sobbing.

The most beautiful relationship she'd ever had, with the most beautiful man she'd ever seen, was over. He was leaving for home next week. For Tennessee. He wasn't interested in a long-distance relationship. He wasn't interested in her.

It was *over* over.

If it had been real to begin with.

One

Presley, dressed smartly in a fuchsia skirt and floral-print blouse and a pair of peep-toe kitten heels, wrapped her folded hands around her knee to keep her leg from bobbing up and down like a sewing machine needle. She was overcaffeinated, thanks to a virtually sleepless night, but when inspiration had struck, she hadn't wanted to waste a single second sleeping.

The smile she'd glued into place was starting to shake at the edges, so she coughed into her hand to give her mouth a rest. When her boss, Delilah, looked up at her again, Presley grinned anew.

Say yes. All I need is a yes.

Presley had longed to escape Florida for as long as she could remember. She'd always wanted to travel the world, visit other countries, meet new and interesting people. But traveling cost money, which had been in short supply. Instead she'd been stuck in Tallahassee as if an invisible force field was keeping her here.

When her boss announced a "friendly" competition for their branch of Viral Pop a month ago, Presley's ears had perked. All she had to do was write an article that would go viral and grab lots of new eyeballs. The winner earned a pay-and-title bump— *hello, Senior Staff Writer!*—and a transfer to any of Viral Pop's offices in the *world*.

Pres had practically foamed at the mouth from excitement. She'd been trying to come up with a winning idea over the last week and a half but nothing came. Until her drive home from work last night, when her ex-boyfriend's song had come on the radio.

Cash Sutherland had left Florida a football star, and was now a country music superstar. Upon hearing his most popular song, a fresh idea had hit her like the title, "Lightning." Out of nowhere and with enough force to split her in two.

Admittedly, she was a tad torn. She didn't relish the idea of revisiting the painful breakup she'd swept under the rug years ago, but on the other hand she really wanted to win. Like, really, *really* wanted to win.

So she'd sat up until 2:00 a.m. last night writing the proposal Delilah was reviewing this very second.

"This would require you to be out of the office," her boss stated, her eyes traveling to Presley. Delilah's usual brand of curiosity-slash-interrogation never failed to intimidate, but winning this promotion and the opportunity to escape Florida was Presley's lifelong dream. She could handle a little intimidation.

"I've worked remotely before," Presley replied. At home, but still. "I am very good at time management. Especially when it's my own time. Or the time here at the office," she was quick to add. "I value your time, as well. More than mine. More than anyone's." She pressed her lips together to keep from sounding desperate, the sticky gloss she'd swiped on this morning helping with that endeavor.

Delilah hummed, set her tablet aside and narrowed her eyelids. Then she dipped her chin. "What makes you so sure Cash Sutherland is going to tell you his biggest songwriting secret when he's dodged that question from every reporter who's spoken with him?"

Nervously, Presley licked her lips. She wasn't *at all* sure Cash Sutherland was going to confess his biggest songwriting secret. Ever since "Lightning" hit the Billboard Top 100, scads of press had been trying to solve the mystery of whom the song was written about. Rumors were rampant. Article after article had named this starlet or that, this singer or the other, and really, given his copious dating history, it could be any *or all* of them.

"We're old friends," she told her boss. "We went to college together. I also visited with his younger brother Gavin to write that article about Elite Records two years ago."

She had no qualms about seeing Cash again. Not really. That long-ago breakup was in the past and she'd done her best to bury it, complete with a tombstone. She had no idea how Cash would feel about her showing up out of the blue, but Gavin had suggested not telling his brother she was coming. "Come to the show," he'd said of the rooftop bar concert Cash was scheduled to play. "Once you're here, he won't have a choice but to talk to you."

Okay, so their plan was a little underhanded, but she couldn't risk Cash turning her away.

During that first visit to Beaumont Bay, she'd made damn sure he was out of the state before scheduling the interview with Gavin and William Sutherland. She hadn't been ready to see Cash then, but couldn't resist chasing the story of how Elite Records had been successfully relaunched by the eldest Sutherland son. She'd been the first to break the news about the resurrected record label in Beaumont Bay. Readers had eaten up the article about four hot brothers in the exciting music town just outside of Nashville.

At the time she'd worried the visit would bring up unpleasant memories, but the lush, rich town hadn't reminded her of the Cash she used to know. She figured she really didn't know him at all. Not anymore.

"It was a small assignment back when I was a content curator," she explained when Delilah didn't comment.

Back then her job had been to compile stories and news to share on social media. Pulling photos and links for articles like "10 Superchic & Supercheap Clothing Finds" wasn't exactly groundbreaking journalism. The piece on Elite Records, the family business run by the Sutherland brothers, gave her a chance to showcase her talents. She'd interviewed Cash's three brothers: producer, Will, lawyer, Gavin, and even bar-owner Luke. She'd mentioned Cash and his accomplishments, if only to appear that she wasn't ignoring his existence entirely, wording it so that it seemed like they'd spoken when in reality they hadn't. That article's success had bumped her status up to staff writer, but she was still chained to her desk in Tallahassee. Lately the most invigorating article she'd written had been titled "10 Times You Wished You Were Taylor Swift."

She was itching to sink her teeth into something juicier.

"Gavin Sutherland told me about a private concert Cash is performing," Presley added. "No other member of the press was invited."

She'd left that nugget out of her proposal, which was mostly a cost analysis showing how inexpensively she could travel—including forgoing the company's per diem. She'd do anything to leave her dinky desk, including paying her own daily expenses. "Elite Records wants to put a positive spin on Cash's DUI and since we know each other, the family trusts me."

Well, Gavin did anyway.

Delilah craned an eyebrow. "Isn't Cash a bad-boy type? Why does he care about a DUI?"

Cash *was* the bad-boy type. Back when they'd dated, he'd shared how he'd stirred up a whole heap of trouble in his hometown of Beaumont Bay. He ran wild as a teen, had once "stolen" his dad's truck to joyride on the back roads. By the time he'd landed a football scholarship to FSU, his parents had breathed a sigh of relief that his days of troublemaking were over.

Now it seemed Cash had returned to his roots—both to his hometown and to his former bad-boy ways. His brothers had even signed him up to tour with good-girl country singer Hannah Banks to help smooth the edges of his otherwise rough reputation.

Cash was a love-'em-and-leave-'em type when it came to women, and Presley knew that from experience. He'd loved and left her when they were in college. Although, "love" was overstating it. Other than a few heavy make-out sessions in her dorm room, they'd never escalated to "love."

Or at least he hadn't.

An inexperienced twentysomething, she'd been completely smitten with him. She'd interviewed Florida State University's unattainable star football player for an assignment, figuring she'd never be closer to him than the six inches separating their seats in the stadium. Color her surprised when he'd asked her to dinner a week later.

She'd been equally surprised when they'd become inseparable. Well, until he left Florida and never spoke to her again. Not only had he left the state and football behind to pursue a music career, but he'd also left her. He'd burned the ships, leaving her with not so much as a life raft.

"Do you think he'll open up to you about the DUI?" her boss asked.

Nooo idea.

"Definitely." Presley nodded. "He's in the process of writing and recording a new album." One that would include a duet featuring Hannah, country music's newest, brightest starlet. "He's going to need the press to help spread the word about the album. He has to know he needs a makeover."

Though not literally. She hadn't bumped into Cash in person in forever, but she'd seen plenty of photos of him online. *Yowza.* He was as beautiful as she remembered. Dark, dark brown hair, golden-brown eyes that sparkled in the sunlight. A strong nose, angled jaw and a smile that could melt the panties off a nun. And that was just above the neck. Add in his height, his rounded, muscular shoulders and biceps, washboard abs and thick, strong thighs and the man was a recipe for an orgasm. In a recent photo, she'd noticed a tattoo on one of his arms. The ink hadn't been there when they'd dated. No doubt one of many changes that had occurred since he'd dumped her.

"I'll give you one week." Delilah slipped her glasses onto her nose and regarded her laptop. A moment later she started typing and Presley wondered if she'd imagined the two words that sounded a lot like approval.

"Was that a…a yes?"

"Yes." Delilah smiled, although it was a few degrees cooler than Presley's own. "I expect a juicy reveal about the woman who inspired 'Lightning,' a deep dive into the bad boy of Beaumont Bay, and the saucy gossip surrounding his DUI. Do you think you can do that?"

"Of course. Absolutely." Presley sprang out of her chair. Delilah's requests sounded a touch invasive, but Presley knew she could write an article that was both informative and respectful. She had no interest in exacting revenge for a breakup that'd occurred eons ago. Her only goal was getting the hell out of Florida.

"And," Delilah said before Presley could escape the office, "I expect you to email your progress to my assistant, Sandra."

"No problem." Presley considered saying something generic like "You can count on me" or "You won't regret this" but decided to save the platitudes. Given her rocky past with Cash, there was a good chance Presley might fail and that Delilah *would* regret sending her on assignment and then realize she *couldn't* count on Presley. She dismissed the thought with a flick of her hair. She'd do everything she could to ensure that didn't happen.

Presley keyed in a text to Gavin Sutherland as she walked through the office to her desk. It read: I leave Friday.

She didn't have to wait long for his response. Perfect. See you then.

Her stomach flopped. She was about to drive eight hours to Tennessee to interview her ex-boyfriend about the women in his past. About a recent DUI. About fame and fortune and his bad-boy ways. *About why he left her.*

Buried past or not, there was a small part of her that longed to know why. Partly for closure, and partly to satisfy her own curiosity. It was a big ask on top of everything else, and she knew that. If she didn't achieve magical "closure" by the time she left, she would console herself with champagne and a first class flight straight out of Tallahassee.

Thankfully, she had the rest of the week to fortify herself for the trip. She hadn't seen him in so long and was already feeling like the younger version of herself. The girl who'd been consumed with him… and then *by* him. She knew better than put herself in that precarious position again.

No, this wouldn't be an easy assignment. But she wasn't missing the opportunity to move up and move on. She'd delayed her dreams for far too long.

Plus, he owed her. He'd left her behind without warning or regret. He was half the reason she'd been trapped in this town to begin with. The internship options she'd considered while they'd dated were in either New York City or Tallahassee. She'd chosen the latter because Cash was in Florida. He'd had a football scholarship and the promise of a professional sports career. He wasn't going anywhere.

Boy, had she been wrong about that.

It was her turn to selfishly focus on her dreams. The title of senior staff writer as well as a position in a Viral Pop office *not* located in Florida awaited her. She could travel to New York, Los Angeles, San Francisco, London…or even Rome. All while keeping her seniority, and without starting over as a new hire at another company. If she loved it, there'd be nothing keeping her from transferring there permanently. Her family could visit, or she could fly home for the holidays. Other than that, she was unattached.

Her heart pattered, keeping time with her fingers as she typed on the keyboard.

She could do this. She *would* do this.

Come Friday, she'd fire up her Jeep and drive to Beaumont Bay to pay her famous ex-boyfriend a visit. She'd draw his secrets from him the same way he'd drawn her into his arms when they'd dated. And, like he had done back then, she'd turn around, drive away and never look back.

A shadow had stretched over Cash Sutherland's life two months ago and it didn't seem to be receding.

He'd hit hard times before, in business and in his personal life, but he'd always sprung back. The reaction from the trolls on social media about his so-called DUI was insane. It was like they were trying to tank his career. The press would do anything for a story.

Vultures.

At the epicenter of the shitstorm was, unsurprisingly, Mags Dumond. The woman had dubbed herself the First Lady of Beaumont Bay years ago when her late husband had been mayor. The Dumond family had founded Beaumont Bay, so he supposed Mags came by the moniker honestly. After a failed attempt at fame in Nashville, Mags had moved back to the Bay, married the mayor and proceeded to host posh parties that'd become a town—and industry—tradition.

The night that would live in infamy for him was the Black & White ball-slash-fundraiser. Everyone who was anyone in the Bay— and that was nearly everyone—had been in attendance. Cash had sipped champagne while milling around in the crowd at the mansion. Around midnight his brothers had begun advancing toward the door and he'd been right behind them. Mags had stopped him, put a drink in his hand and insisted on a toast. After a final cheers, and taking a single sip of the drink he didn't want, Cash climbed behind the wheel of his Bugatti Chiron.

He'd *felt* sober when he happened upon the random sobriety checkpoint in the short jaunt from Mags's hilltop mansion to his countryside house. But according to the officer who pulled him over, Cash had been one-tenth of a point over the legal limit.

The memory of the whole evening chafed him. Mags had harassed him much of the night, a habit she'd perfected over time, and one he'd grown tired of. She'd been pressuring him to sign with her record label, Cheating Hearts, for years. The company was her pride and joy—and the result of her own lost dreams of stardom. While Mags was failing at becoming a singer, Eleanor Banks—Hannah's grandmother—had become Nashville's sweetheart. Tail tucked, Mags returned to the Bay and fell in love. The mayor had promised her the world, and purchased a record label for her.

When Cash's brother Will relaunched well-respected Elite Records, Mags hadn't hid her resentment. She'd made it clear that the Sutherland boys were traipsing on hallowed ground. No one had the audacity to compete with the queen of the Bay. That is, until Will had taken on Elite, Cash recorded an album with the label and subsequently won the industry's top award. There was no stopping Elite's success now that Will's fiancée, Hannah, was on board. Plus, their brother Luke had launched many a new performer's career by inviting them to play at one of his bars and Gavin, a music attorney, worked exclusively with Elite Record artists.

Town and industry history aside, the only history that mattered now was the fact that Cash's mug shot was decorating the internet like the toilet paper he'd once strung into the trees outside of his high school. His angry expression in the photo made him appear guilty—or, if the Breathalyzer could be trusted, guilt*ier*.

Up until that point, he'd been a bad boy with an unstoppable lucky streak. First, a hit album, then awards, soon a new tour and album with Hannah to solidify his new status, and then *the world*. A public shaming pulled the emergency brake on those plans.

While his biggest fans supported him, his corporate sponsors hadn't been as loyal. A famous shoe brand canceled his contract and following that, a popular game app he'd already filmed a commercial for let him know they would not air it. Suddenly "the bad boy of country music," who'd filled stadiums to capacity last summer, had been labeled unsafe for public consumption.

His mind a million miles from where it should be, he finished singing the final note of the song into the microphone.

Behind the glass of his at-home studio, his oldest brother, Will, stood, arms folded, a scowl on his face. His brother's scowl had taken up residency years ago, but had receded some after he'd begun dating Hannah. Cash had thought those two would've been oil and water, but it turned out they had a lot in common and had fallen in love. His stoic, powerful, rigid brother in love with an explosive rainbow of color and energy like Hannah Banks? It was the stuff of fairy tales. Which was what romantic love was to Cash. A fairy tale.

Will, behind soundproof glass, pressed a button so Cash could hear him. "I'd say go again but you should save your voice for the concert on Friday night." He made a wrap-up motion and Cash pulled off his headphones.

"Can't wait," Cash grumbled to himself. The concert on Friday night was a publicity stunt. He was not thrilled. When he'd imagined a shiny new career as a beloved music artist, he'd expected to glide through each and every day doing what he loved. He'd walked away from football, college, and worse—his girlfriend at the time, Presley. He'd convinced himself that breaking her heart would be worth it for both of them.

As far as Pres was concerned, he knew she was working for a huge media conglomerate. Her article on Elite a few years back seemed to do well and had painted the Sutherlands in a favorable light. Clearly, she'd moved on. He had too, though it'd been ten times harder than he'd imagined it would.

He loved performing, loved to hang with fans, but the rest of his duties could be exhausting. Living his passion came with a heap of bullshit like marketing, interviews with reporters and a recent press conference where he'd publicly apologized for being drunk when he damn well wasn't.

Cash rested his guitar on its stand, bypassing Will, who was studying his phone.

"Want to grab dinner?" Will asked. "Gavin and Luke are at Silver Marmot."

Not one to turn down filet mignon and lobster, Cash nodded. It'd been a long day. A long *month*.

"You'll be all right," Will encouraged as they walked upstairs and through Cash's house en route to the front door. "The aftermath of DUIs don't last forever."

No, it just felt like it.

Cash wanted to believe Friday night's performance would be the magic bullet that erased everyone's memory of his mug shot, but he knew better. While it might not last "forever" as his brother said, it could shadow them for months to come. Or years.

God help him.

For his brothers' sakes, Cash hoped recouping wasn't far off. Elite Records didn't need the bad press, either.

"Want me to drive?" Will stroked the hood of Cash's ice-blue Bugatti, its sparkling paint glittering in the setting sunlight.

"No way your ass is touching the driver's seat of my baby." Cash unlocked the doors and slid in. "Not like I'll be drinking alcohol tonight anyway."

And in public, possibly never again.

Two

Presley arrived in Beaumont Bay much later than she intended, after nine hours of road-tripping, traffic-sitting and rest-stopping. She dashed into the Beaumont Hotel, a dress protected by a plastic dry-cleaning bag draped over her forearm, and past a few bodies in the lobby on her way to the ladies' room. She shouldn't care about what Cash thought of her driving outfit, but there was no way was she interviewing her ex while wearing stretch pants and an oversize T-shirt.The hotel was as luxe as she'd expected, with huge columns and marble flooring, patterned rugs and clerks dressed in white shirts with smart black vests and pants.

She'd planned to arrive a few hours before the rooftop concert being held in this very hotel, but Fate had other plans. At least Gavin had tipped her off about the service elevator, a secret passage of sorts that would take her to the venue without her having to file upstairs with ticketed guests.

She changed in one of the bathroom stalls and then regarded her reflection in the attached sitting room, pausing for a scant second to absorb what she was seeing. The room was large, furnished with a pair of stuffed chairs and a settee. A glass table with a carafe of coffee was available for guests.

It's the Taj Ma-Powder Room.

After brushing her teeth and freshening her makeup, she made quick work of finger-combing her auburn hair, which had wilted from the heat of the day. She hadn't dared take the top off her Jeep, and was glad for the decision now. She'd driven through a hell of a rainstorm.

She tucked the dry-cleaning bag into the trash can and rolled her driving clothes into a wad before stuffing them into her bag. As she was preparing to walk out, a woman entered, a cacophony of voices following her in from the lobby.

Presley recognized the slightly desperate, demanding tone of the press when she heard it. She stepped aside to let the woman pass and then burst into the lobby, her purse on her shoulder as she waded into a sea of people.

Men and women with long-lens cameras, and others with cell phones in hand, shot photos and video of their subject. The one, the only—

"Cash Sutherland!" one reporter shouted. "Cash!"

A few others tried their luck with "Over here! Cash!" and at least one went the lowbrow route of inquiring loudly about his DUI.

Tacky.

Presley pushed through the crowd, catching sight of the top of Cash's dark head, eyes hidden behind sunglasses, mouth a grim line.

Her world froze.

He was even grander in person than in her memory—and far more potent than his photos online. Memories threatened to surface, but she shoved them down as she wedged her way through the crowd. Memories would slow her down. If she wanted her life to finally begin moving—if she wanted to travel to places beyond her hometown—she needed to focus on the future, not the past.

An opening cleared thanks to a bellman trying to help with crowd control. Presley nestled in near a woman waving a concert T-shirt in the air. Cash scribbled his name on the shirt with a black marker before handing it back to her, never spotting Presley. The woman gazed longingly at her prize and Presley took advantage, slinking between her and the bellman to chase after Cash. A security guard just missed her, holding up his arms and shouting to the crowd to "give Mr. Sutherland some space!"

Sorry, Mr. Sutherland, ain't gonna happen.

She skirted the front desk and caught up to a clerk shooing Cash into the service elevator. When the clerk nearly plowed into her, he frowned. She beamed up at the waifish man, her smile at full wattage.

"Thank you so much." She pressed a hand to her chest. "I nearly lost him in the crowd. It was terrifying."

The clerk waved her through, either not knowing she'd lied about arriving with the singer, or not caring. Just as Cash pressed a button on the panel on the elevator, she slipped inside. The doors whispered shut behind her, caging them in—literally since three of the walls were outfitted with iron bars over glass with a view of the elevator shaft.

"What the hell—" he started, his thick eyebrows lowering over his nose. Then his anger faded into surprise.

His low voice skipped over each and every one of her vertebrae, sending chills through her limbs even in the stuffy elevator car. She tried to speak but her tongue wouldn't work while in such close proximity to the man who used to turn her inside out with merely a look.

He blinked. "Presley?"

In spite of every pep talk she'd given herself before this assignment, her mind wandered back to how his broad hands felt on her body. To how his firm lips used to turn her inside out. He'd given her more than one orgasm without kissing her below the waist. It'd been the thrill of her life at the time. Sadly, it still might be.

"Hi." She licked her lips, preparing to say more,

but the elevator car bumped and jerked like they'd boarded an amusement park ride instead. She grabbed hold of the nearest solid surface, in this case, stacks of glassware in large plastic racks destined for the bar.

Cash also gripped the rack of glasses, and her eyes moved from those long, talented fingers to his attractive hands and then up his arm to the ink that vanished into the sleeve of a black T-shirt.

There it was. The tattoo of music notes wrapping around a guitar she'd seen in photos. Or part of it anyway. Half of the colorful design was hidden.

The elevator jerked again, but rather than complete its ascent to the roof it bumped and whined in place. Overhead, the lights flickered.

"Service elevators. Yikes," she said to break the silence.

Cash was not amused. She wasn't sure if the fluorescent lights were to blame, but he appeared slightly green in color. A fine sheen of sweat coated his upper lip. His knuckles, wrapped tightly around the rack of glasses, stood out in stark contrast from the rest of his tanned skin.

"Are you… Are you okay?"

He didn't answer, his eyes turning to the ceiling where the light flickered again. His nostrils flared, the column of his throat moving as if he was trying to swallow a bowling ball.

"Cash?" She moved to touch him but he sliced her in two with a hard glare.

His voice a low warning, he growled, "What the hell do you think you're doing?"

Presley didn't hesitate answering, but whatever she was saying was coming at him like they were underwater. Or buried in wet cement.

The only sounds he could concentrate on were the whine of the elevator cables, the stacked glassware rattling away beneath his white-knuckled grip, and the concrete shaft visible through the iron-and-glass walls surrounding him. Who's bright idea had that been?

He rode elevators *never* if he could help it. He'd been stuck in one with his mother when he was five years old. They'd sat sweating in that box for what had felt like days, but Dana Sutherland assured him it'd been a "mere forty minutes" before help had arrived.

There was nothing "mere" about forty minutes trapped in a vertical coffin if you asked him. The only reason he was in this godforsaken cracker box on cables was because hoofing it up flights upon flights of stairs right before he went on stage would affect his performance.

And not in a good way.

Presley hadn't taken kindly to him asking what the hell she was doing. She was answering him, in a clipped, sharp tone and with plenty of gesticulating. He supposed he shouldn't be surprised by her reaction. Seeing him for the first time since he'd left her crying in Florida likely hadn't filled her with warm fuzzies.

He'd wondered if she'd forgiven him for leaving her. Considering the sparks that shot through her blue eyes, he guessed the answer was no.

She looked different from how he remembered her, but also the same. She had the same fire-red hair, and the same delicate freckles dotting the bridge her nose. Her black dress was more professional than party-girl, but no less tantalizing. Presley Cole had always been gorgeous. Still was.

"...not to mention I drove all the way from Tallahassee to *help you*," she was saying. "You're welcome."

"Help me," he repeated between clenched teeth. At least arguing took his mind off their predicament. "With what?"

"With your DUI, you idiot. There are a hundred reporters downstairs, and if you think a single one of them would give you the benefit of the doubt about your drunk driving—"

"I wasn't drunk," he snapped.

"Tell that to the judge."

"I did." The elevator jerked, Cash's stomach along with it. Before he could do something seriously emasculating, like yip, Presley lost her balance and touched him. It was an innocent forearm grab, but her painted pink nails and the pale freckles on her arm reminded him of times not so innocent. Times he'd unhooked her bra before kissing her chest. Times he'd flicked open the stud on her jeans and slipped his hand inside…

Snap out of it.

"You're here for an interview?" he asked.

"Yes. For Viral Pop. It's a huge media conglomerate."

He knew all about Viral Pop. It was a step sideways from the gossip magazines.

"No interview," he growled, desperately trying to pull himself together.

"Oh, you're granting me an interview." Her laugh showcased high cheekbones, her eyes, as blue as the Gulf Stream, flickering in challenge.

"Not even if we're trapped in this rickety tuna can for the remainder of the evening," he told her, his stomach souring at the thought of being stuck in here. This was his worst nightmare come true.

Her arm shot out and her hand slammed the emergency stop button. The elevator lurched to a halt and a buzzy alarm began blaring.

"Listen here, Mr. Big Shot. As I have it tallied, you owe me at least a few minutes of your precious time. I'm not here uninvited, by the way. Gavin understands how a positive spin on your recent crisis could help you, and the record label." She searched the inside of the elevator with obvious impatience. "How do I turn the alarm off?"

"You don't." He swiped his brow with the back of his hand, feeling woozier than before. This was just what he fucking needed. His ex-girlfriend, looking as hot as he remembered, yelling at him in an elevator stuck between floors.

"Cash, seriously. Are you okay?" Her harsh tone gentled as her other hand joined the first on his arm.

Stunning blue eyes inventoried his face, and the elevator walls faded. He recalled, with frightening clarity, the feel of her mouth on his, the way their tongues tangled as he plucked her nipple into a turgid peak. She'd orgasmed from that alone. He'd loved hearing her sweet cries in his ears while she tugged on his hair. His good girl, shirt rucked up, bra on the floor.

Yeah, his minor bout of claustrophobia was competing with another sensation entirely. Like the semi stirring to life behind his fly. She'd been polite and careful and as sweet as saltwater taffy back when they'd dated. Now, he sensed that same sweetness, but she'd added pure fire to the mix. Concern mingled with curiosity in her eyes. She was still touching him. Her black dress hugged demure curves, making him remember all he'd seen—and tasted— underneath.

The speaker crackled and a voice announced itself as "Rod from Maintenance." Presley looked over her shoulder at the panel, then turned back to Cash, a question forming on her pursed lips.

He didn't let her ask it. Instead, he leaned down and captured her plush mouth with a firm, unyielding kiss.

Three

Presley was fairly certain she was having an out-of-body experience.

Or maybe the elevator had plummeted several stories and she'd died and gone to heaven. Considering how amazing Cash's mouth felt on hers, she couldn't dismiss the possibility outright.

She'd shut her eyes, so the rest of her senses were on high alert. She moved her hands to his biceps, brushing her thumbs over solid muscle beneath smooth flesh. His mouth was firm and warm, and when his tongue touched hers, she lost the strength in her knees.

He must have noticed because next he steadied her with his hands. Oh, those talented hands. How had she forgotten? They were talented at strumming a guitar and *really* talented at turning her on. His lips still on hers, his fingers tightened around her waist and he tugged her close. Her breasts flattened on his chest, but when she lifted her arms to capture his neck, she lost his mouth.

His gaze was hazy, almost shell-shocked, as he sucked in a gulp of air. She did the same, unable to tear her eyes from the perfect vision of Cash up close. Dark scruff surrounded his luscious mouth, his lips damp from their kisses. Long eyelashes shadowed golden-brown eyes that appeared darker in the meager light.

He broke the spell by swearing. *Loudly.*

Setting her body aside, he went to the panel on the elevator, pressed a button, spoke to the crackling voice and then pressed another button.

Her heartbeat sloshed noisily in her ears as she descended to earth, still tingling from the kiss she hadn't even tried to stop. Which made no sense, as she was completely over him. *Completely*, she silently reminded herself.

The elevator started with a jerk and she gripped the rack of glasses to steady herself, her knees still weak.

You know, from making out with him.

Cash faced the doors for the remainder of the short ride. He sent her a dark look over his shoulder when the elevator opened on the rooftop. His last words to her were "Gavin, really?"

"What's that supposed to mean?" she mumbled. To herself, since he was no longer anywhere around.

She stepped into the bar, angry, but mostly with herself. Yes, he'd kissed her first, but she'd kissed him *back*.

On her long list of "things to do" while visiting Beaumont Bay, kissing her ex wasn't on it. She'd once been weak for him. She couldn't let herself be that weak again.

She understood why Gavin had suggested not telling Cash about the interview ahead of time. Cash definitely hadn't been happy to see her.

The kiss hadn't been an "I want you" or an "I missed you." No, it'd been about something else. For her, an unwelcome visit from her past. For Cash, who was moving damn fast in black cowboy boots, the kiss had acted like a release valve on a pressurized container.

The posh, luxe bar was half indoors, half out. Shining wood floors stretched through the interior, couches and chairs surrounding low tables with lit candles. The bar was more like a really large living room. Outside, the patio's high glass walls offered a view of the city buildings and lake and trees beyond. Golden hour was upon them, bathing the stage where Cash would perform tonight in a warm, buttery light.

She walked in that direction, but a beefy security guy held up one massive mitt. "I don't think so, lady."

She opened her mouth to shout Cash's name. He had some explaining to do. Namely, why he'd kissed

her and run away. Before she could, Gavin Sutherland materialized in front of her.

"It's okay, Irv, she's with us." Gavin's warm smile
was a welcome sight. "Welcome to the Cheshire bar.
How are you, Pres?"

What a question.

"Late." She adjusted the bag on her shoulder.

"Nah, you're fine. You took my advice about the
service elevator, I assume?"

"Yeah." That'd been a bang-up plan, hadn't it?

Two years ago, when she'd visited Beaumont Bay
for the Elite Records interview, she hadn't known
what to expect. She knew she wouldn't run into Cash
since he'd been on tour and was somewhere on the
East Coast—North Carolina if she remembered
right. But she hadn't been sure what his youngest
brother, Gavin, would be like.

Turned out Gavin was open and easy to talk to.
He was kind, and reminded her of the Cash in her
memory—the one who had been running toward
her briefly before he ran away.

A habit he'd never fully kicked, it seemed.

"Don't worry about Irv. He's just doing his job.
I'll grab you a backstage pass later." Gavin placed
a hand on her lower back and guided her away from
the stage. He was a looker, from his contagious smile
to the open-placket white button-down shirt. "How
about a cocktail?"

"That would be great." As handsome and kind as
he was, she didn't feel the same ripple of attraction
as she felt for Cash. Which was alarming since she

wasn't supposed to be feeling anything for Cash. "It's pretty empty up here. I'd have thought he'd pack the place."

"We don't open the doors for another fifteen minutes. How's the lobby looking?"

"Like a shark tank with chum in the water." She smiled when Gavin laughed.

"I noticed Cash rushing in like his ass was on fire. He's usually late, but not this late. Wonder what the holdup was?"

She knew, but she wasn't saying.

"He's never been much for rehearsal. Likes to be spontaneous."

"So I've gathered," she said under her breath.

Gavin gestured to a female bartender wearing a leather vest, an exposed red bra beneath it. A streak of red decorated her blond hair. "Christy, can you shake up something special for Presley while I fetch her a backstage pass? She's a friend of the family so put whatever she wants on my tab."

"Sure thing, hon." Christy's eyes crinkled at the corners, hinting she was a touch older than her outfit suggested. "How about a Lightning Bolt, sweetheart? It's Cash Sutherland's signature drink."

"Named after his famous song, 'Lightning,' I presume."

"The one and only. The girls go wild for that song—and the drink."

Just what she needed. But, what the hell. "Sure. Why not?"

Turned out the Cash Sutherland's signature drink

was blue and fruity…and served in a martini glass with a cherry in the bottom. Which had her musing about her own intact virginity back when she'd dated him, and the likely color of his balls as they took things far, but never went all the way.

Her stomach rolled, regret and relief switching places, but she thanked Christy for the drink anyway.

Boots hooked on the rungs of a stool backstage, Cash concentrated on tuning his guitar while the band readied their instruments. He'd assumed tonight's set would be as rote as they came, given they'd performed it at least once in every state in the country, and in several countries outside the United States. Then again, after what'd happened in the service elevator, anything being "rote" tonight was a big assumption.

He hummed as he plucked the strings, his mind not on his music but on every agonizing, skin-tightening, ball-seizing second of kissing Presley in that elevator. Her truncated breaths, the feel of her small hands on his arms as she sealed her body to his. The incredibly confident way her mouth moved beneath his, slanting when he would have backed off, diving deeper when he *should have* backed off.

They'd been kids when they'd dated—her nineteen-going-on-twenty to his should've-known-better twenty-three. But she wasn't nineteen-going-on-twenty any longer. She was thirty to his thirty-three, and his sweet Presley had bloomed. Sneaking into that elevator and implying she was here to save his career was not the Presley he remembered.

Cash would strangle his younger brother for keeping this from him.

"Set list, boss." Mikey, his bassist, handed over a sheet of paper.

Cash reviewed it, nodded and handed it back. Mikey taped it to the floor next to the microphone stand and ambled off to finish setting up.

Cash didn't know how the hell he was supposed to perform "Lightning" knowing Presley was out there watching—and preparing to report on—his every move. Especially after the kiss that had stopped the world. And the elevator.

He was used to the wolves coming for him in the form of paparazzi and press, but the last person he'd expected to take advantage of his fame was her. She had shown up a few years back to interview his family, without so much as an email to alert him. Not that he blamed her for not contacting him. Not after how things ended between them…how *he'd* ended things.

He'd been a senior at the time, itching to finish school or drop out entirely. He didn't care, so long as college was *over*. If it hadn't been for a football scholarship, he never would have gone to Florida. Never would have met Presley Cole. At the moment, he couldn't decide if that would have been better.

Anyway, he'd broken his finger on the field, an injury that had since healed but still caused him pain after a long show or hours of practice. He hadn't been able to play football immediately following, which was a huge relief, but he also hadn't been able to hold a pen or play guitar, and that had been the ultimate deal breaker.

His dad, Travis, had high hopes for Cash to play for the NFL. Cash hadn't wanted to live out his father's dream. He'd had his own dream. The decision to leave Florida State was easy. Leaving his budding relationship with Presley was not.

The break from football gave him a lot of perspective. He saw how he'd influenced Presley and not in a positive way. More than once, she'd broken curfew while they'd dated. She'd gone to parties she had no business being at, and had skipped hanging with her friends to watch him play ball.

She hadn't been the only one affected negatively by their relationship. He'd done his share of skipping class, sleeping in after spending the night with her in his arms. He'd respected her wishes not go all the way sexually during their heavy make-out sessions, but wanting her had become a type of torture the longer they were together.

She'd probably never know how much it'd gutted him to give her the "it's not you it's me" breakup speech. To watch her eyes fill with tears and then walk away like he didn't care. He had cared. Way too much.

After he'd decided to stop chasing his father's dream and chase his own for a change, Cash knew what coming home to Tennessee meant. It meant dedicating all his time to succeeding, and that hadn't left any time for Presley.

When he broke up with her, he'd reminded her that she had big dreams of her own. To be a writer, to travel. He knew she'd turned down an internship in NYC to stay close to him. The last thing he wanted was for her not to follow her own dreams in exchange for being with him. But in reality, he hadn't been as magnanimous as he'd made himself out to be. He'd been selfish, and she deserved better. Then and now.

Sad as it was, their brief relationship, honest and loving at the start, heartbreaking and lonely at the end, made for great country music fodder.

Too bad the song he'd written to help him get over her only seemed to reopen the wound every time he sang it.

"Ten minutes," Mikey called out.

Cash nodded that he was ready. If there was one thing he could do it was compartmentalize. And as far as pushing thoughts of Presley into the past went, well, he'd had a hell of a lot of practice.

Four

No wonder the man won awards.

Presley was sitting at a high-top table with Gavin and a few of his friends, trying not to stare at Cash. She failed when he performed his signature song. And she wasn't the only one who couldn't tear her eyes off him. A reverent hush fell over the crowd and goose bumps chilled her arms as he sang "Lightning."

Cash had been the one to encourage her to follow her dreams of becoming a journalist and traveling the world. She should probably thank him. Once he'd left Florida, she became focused entirely on her schoolwork. She'd put relationships on the back burner, spending more time with her laptop than she ever had a boy. In a way, losing Cash had galvanized her. She'd become bulletproof since. Or so she'd thought before he sang the knife-twist final line of his biggest hit.

How I wish, oh how I wish, lightning struck twice.

There was a sacred pause between the strum of the last chord and the audience erupting in applause. Slightly stunned, she joined in and clapped, as well. That hour had flown.

"What now?" one of the women at their table asked. "Do we rush the stage and tear his clothes off?"

Gavin laughed. "I'd love to see you try. Go for it."

The woman and her friend laughed and then dared each other to do it. Presley's stomach twisted into a knot. She wasn't sure if she was feeling melancholy that she'd had access to quite a bit of Cash's body back in the day, or jealous that other women had access to it now.

"You okay, Pres?" Gavin asked, and she remembered that she was supposed to be.

"Yep! Does he come out and mingle now?"

The crowd was small, but there were enough drooling women to form a mob if they banded together. Currently, one woman was begging for a peek backstage while the burly security guy's head swept left and right like a pendulum.

"Not usually," Gavin answered. "Even an intimate crowd can be rowdy. Women go nuts for him."

"Yeah," Presley mumbled, disappointed to learn that her reaction to him was far from unique.

"He'll come out after a majority of the crowd has dispersed. Usually we meet up in the VIP lounge.

Luke's probably already back there. Will and Hannah were planning on coming out, too."

"Hannah Banks. Right." Country music megastar and a surprising match for the most serious of the Sutherland brothers. "I look forward to meeting her."

"You'll like her. You know, you're good with fame." Gavin sounded amused. He sipped from his lowball glass. "Is it because you knew Cash from way-back-when, or does your line of work make fame commonplace?"

"Bit of both." She shrugged. "Celebrities are people. And you can't be a blithering idiot if you want to interview them successfully. You have to play it cool."

She nearly burst out laughing at herself. Yes, she'd played it *soooo* cool when she'd slipped into an elevator with Cash and then tangled her tongue with his.

Anyway. She cleared her throat.

"Let's go to the VIP lounge now and ditch the masses," Gavin suggested. "You down for some gourmet fried appetizers?"

Fluttering her lashes, she touched her décolletage. "You had me at *fried.*"

They sidestepped a cluster of people who were pressing toward the stage, drawn in by Cash's ridiculously universal appeal. She passed two women who were crying and saying they'd "give anything to meet him."

Been there. Done that. Burned one of his T-shirts.

She hadn't known what she was walking into

when she'd dated him years ago, but she did now. At one point she'd given up an internship to New York City to stay close to him, something she'd grown to regret. Leaving him had been unthinkable. He hadn't shared her feelings.

Well, it wasn't like she had come here to re-kindle their relationship. She was here to find out who "Lightning" had been written about, and then share that news in an exclusive article that would go *so* viral Viral Pop would be tempted to name the company after her. In other words, she had a job to do and she intended to do it well. Being distracted by Cash's incredible...*everything* was not on the agenda.

In the VIP lounge, Gavin led her to a roped-off area where Will Sutherland stood, his nose in Hannah Banks's blond hair. She was more gorgeous in person, especially since she was grinning ear to ear. When Will emerged from her locks, so was he.

Ah, love.

At one point, Presley had thought she was in love with Cash. Now she knew better. What the women in this crowd—and at least one guy—felt for the singer was adoration, and had nothing to do with "love."

She understood now that she'd been caught up in adoration, too. Cash had been an incredible quarter-back who could play the guitar and sing any woman into an orgasm. He had an irresistibility about him that, unfortunately, hadn't gone anywhere.

But resist him she would.

Once upon a time, he had been singularly focused

on his own career and damn the consequences. Now it was her turn to nurture her career and leave him in the dust. Granted, she wasn't very good at being selfish, but hey, maybe Cash could give her a few pointers while she was here.

Five

Cash sucked in a breath through flared nostrils and kept his carefully trained half smile in place while the woman in front of him tried to keep from sobbing. She was happy—he assumed—but it was hard to tell when both a cry and a laugh overlapped.

"I...j-just wanted to tell you that y-your music changed my life and that I luh-love you. I love you s-so much."

This was the most uncomfortable part of meeting fans. He thought he'd be used to this sort of display by now, but for him it never got any easier.

"I appreciate that, Tabitha," he said in a low, soothing voice.

Her eyes widened, lashes blinking away tears as she grinned. When he'd first begun performing, women like Tabitha had flattered his pants off. Literally, in some cases. Thankfully he pulled his head out of his backside before he became a regular with the groupies.

Those hookups had been less satisfying than they were awkward, for both parties. He'd stuck with actual relationships instead, though he kept them short. That way he could take care of the physical ache while avoiding the "what was your name again?" conversation the next morning.

"Time's up, miss." Irv, who ran security for the Cheshire, was large, slightly frightening and gruff. In other words, exactly what Cash needed. He winked at Tabitha and told her to have a good night. Then he and Irv moved as one through the bar until Cash was deposited in the VIP lounge.

Safe at last.

Then he spotted Presley talking with Hannah and thought maybe he wasn't safe. She had tried to kill him, after all. If not by pressing the emergency button that stopped the elevator, then with the kiss that damn near stopped his heart.

Her blue eyes sparked like flint striking stone as he stepped into the room. She wasn't happy with him, though he didn't know if that was because of recent events or their shared past.

Hannah, her hand linked with Will's, turned for the bar. His brother gave him a nod of greeting and Hannah smiled her perfect, pearly smile. Cash liked her, always had. It wouldn't be a hardship touring with her when the time came. Both Hannah and her twin sister, Hallie, were from the best kind of stock. Their grandmother, Eleanor, had raised them right.

Presley wasn't glaring at him any longer. She had decided to ignore him completely. From her perch on a plush red sofa, she grinned at his brother Gavin, who had just returned with a drink for each of them. Cash could deck his younger brother for inviting his ex-girlfriend to Beaumont Bay without telling him. Whose side was he on?

"You two are looking cozy," Cash said. "Though you've been in touch lately, so that makes sense."

"Ignore King High and Mighty, Pres," Gavin told her, unfazed by Cash's surly entry.

"No worries. I do." She flashed a tight smile Cash's way and he gave her the practiced half smile he reserved for fans.

"Beer, Mr. Sutherland?" A cocktail waitress approached. She was new if he wasn't mistaken.

In a town like Beaumont Bay, luxury and high-class living were the norm. It was unique for staff to stick around anywhere for long. Not that Cash frequented his brother's bar, but when he was here, he wasn't used to seeing the same friendly staff. Jobs around here were a means to an end, and once the fame-seeker found his or her opening, they left faster than you could say, "I'd love a beer." Which was what he told the waitress now.

"What kind?" She peeked flirtatiously through her lashes.

He grinned. "Surprise me."

She turned and wiggled away, making her classy black pantsuit look a hell of a lot more scandalous.

"Wow." Presley raised her auburn eyebrows. "You *can* be charming."

"Presley!" Hannah called from the bar. "Come over here. There's someone I want you to meet!"

Hallie, Hannah's identical twin sister, stood between Hannah and Will. Hallie was a carbon copy of her famous sister. Blonde and beautiful with bright hazel eyes and a wide mouth. They were easy to tell apart. Hallie wore a neutral beige dress, her hair tied back in a low ponytail, while Hannah practically glowed in a bright pink dress covered in twinkling rhinestones. Those two definitely had their differences.

"If you'll excuse me," Presley said sweetly. To Gavin.

When she was gone, Cash took her seat as the waitress delivered his beer. "Thanks, honey."

She didn't hover, which he appreciated. He took a long draw. Damn, that tasted good. He wasn't a big drinker, but it was tradition to enjoy a beer after a performance. By his calculations, he'd more than earned one.

"You want to tell me why Presley Cole is here yammering about interviewing me about my DUI?"

Gavin took a swallow from his gin and tonic and pretended to think about it. "No. I don't think I will."

"What are you not saying?"

"I know how you feel about the press, but when it comes to clearing your name with the public, she can help you."

Cash doubted her motivations were that noble.

"Your expression doesn't exactly scream that you're on board," Gav said with a grin. "Look, Pres wrote an article about Elite Records that was not only well written, it was fair. She didn't misquote Will, or play up a rivalry between Mags Dumond and the Sutherlands like *Rolling Stone* did."

Cash frowned. He recalled that magazine article. It'd had a ripple effect on social media that took a long while to peter out. If he disliked the press, he *hated* social media.

"She called a few weeks back asking if the studio had recovered from the storm, and we talked about your DUI. I told her it was trumped-up bullshit and she said she could've guessed and offered to help clear your name." Gavin shrugged. "She's on our side, Cash. And the timing is perfect since you're recording a new album. She can mention that alongside how Elite Records rose from the ashes after the storm nearly flattened it. Two birds. One stone."

"Your metaphors need work," Cash grumbled before returning to his point. "She's my ex-girlfriend and you should've told me."

"You dated her a hundred years ago."

"Did it occur to you she could be here to exact revenge on me for breaking up with her?" Cash asked under his breath after checking to make sure no one was listening. He could never be too careful.

Gavin leaned in. "Did it occur to *you* how it's a miracle this VIP lounge can hold both you *and* your enormous ego?"

Jerk.

"Revenge. Do you hear yourself?" His brother shook his head. "She's as sweet as apple pie."

Cash knew for a fact that she tasted equally sweet. He ground his molars together. Gavin wasn't stupid enough to flirt with her, but Cash delivered a threat anyway. "As wholesome as apple pie too. So, mind yourself."

Gavin couldn't comment since Presley returned at that moment. Cash moved down the couch to give her seat back, regretting it when she sat closer to Gavin than him.

"Hallie is so nice," Presley said. "Shy, though. I guess it's poor form to assume twins have the same personality. They are individuals."

"She's been around a lot more since Will and Hannah have been together, but she barely says two words to me." Gavin sounded slightly stung.

And Gavin thought *Cash* was the one with the ego? Gav hated when people didn't like him— women in particular.

"I wonder why? You're so easy to talk to." Presley touched Gavin's leg. Clearly Cash's kiss hadn't been more than a blip on her radar if she was already flirting with his brother.

"I'm taking off," Cash announced abruptly. He'd seen enough. He set his unfinished beer on the table in front of the couch and stood.

"Pres is staying the week," Gavin said, his smile not at all innocent. "You should give her a full tour while she's here."

* * *

Cash's expression matched Presley's scowl, though he looked more comfortable wearing it than she felt.

"Where are you staying?" Gavin asked her.

"The Rose Something. In Greencamp?" When the name didn't spark recognition in either of them, she thumbed through her phone for the confirmation email. "Oh, here it is. The Dusty Rose."

"No," Gavin said at the same time Cash said, "Absolutely not."

"Well, the Beaumont—" she gestured around at the lush bar perched atop the hotel "—while quite lovely, is a *wee* smidge outside of my budget."

And Viral Pop's. While funds were *not* a problem for the Sutherland family, she was here partially on her own dime. The credit card she'd been given for "expenses" had a limit that was hilarious. But she was willing to dip into her savings to fund this trip, figuring that the pay raise after she won the contest would refill it and then some. Staying in Beaumont Bay proper wouldn't be dipping into her savings, it'd be scraping it dry.

Gavin and Cash exchanged dark glances and she shifted in her seat.

"Should I check into somewhere closer? There wasn't much occupancy in neighboring towns given it's summer at the lake."

"You're right about that," Gavin said. "Occupancy is an issue right now, but the Dusty Rose isn't where you want to stay."

"It looked charming. And it's only a half an hour up the road."

"On those back-country roads, it'll take longer than that. And you can bet the Dusty Rose is about as charming as my brother." Gavin smirked, proud of the jab.

"I'm more charming than black mold and roaches," Cash commented.

Presley cringed. "It's that bad?"

"Yes," the brothers agreed.

"You can stay with me," Gavin said. "Free of charge."

"With you?" she and Cash asked in chorus. Except her tone was curious and his was…something else.

"Why would she stay with you if she's here to talk to me?" Cash snapped, suddenly defending the very interview he swore he wouldn't allow.

"Because *I* invited her here."

"Your apartment is the size of the elevator Pres and I rode up here in," Cash continued arguing. She didn't miss Gavin's sideways glance. Heat spread over her chest and climbed her neck as she relived what happened in the cramped space. "What are you going to do, share a bathroom?"

"Really, the hotel is fine," she tried interjecting.

"Cash's house is bigger than mine, but only because my *bigger*, *nicer* house is currently being built. I'm in temporary quarters right now," Gavin explained. "But, his place is on the lake. So while you'd be staying with the grouchiest Sutherland in Beaumont Bay, the view might be worth it."

"And I have a guest wing."

"Guest *rooms*. He's exaggerating." Gavin rolled his eyes. "But they are nice. I've stayed there a time or two."

"Uh…" What a choice. She could either add in extra travel time and risk roaches and black mold at the Dusty Rose, suffer a bit of awkwardness by staying—and sharing a bathroom—with Gavin, or stay in "the guest wing" of her sexy ex-boyfriend's lakefront house. Plus, if she wasn't mistaken, Cash had just agreed to the interview. "If you're sure it's not an inconvenience. I can pay you if—"

"Absolutely not," Cash repeated, then looked at his brother. "It's settled. She's staying with me."

Why, oh why, did his claiming her send a shiver of awareness down her spine?

"You'd better get going, then." Gavin clapped Cash's shoulder. "Make sure there are clean sheets on the guest bed."

Cash sent his brother one final dark look before pulling out his phone. It buzzed in his hand. "Looks like Rickie's already there anyway."

"His agent," Gavin explained to Presley.

"What's your phone number?" Cash asked her. "I'll text you the address. Then you'll have my number so you can call if you get lost."

She rattled off her cell phone number and Cash punched it into his phone before making his escape. She watched his confident swagger, unsure how she'd started off with hotel reservations and ended up agreeing to bunking with Cash.

Well, not *with him*. But in his house.

"You sure you're okay staying with him?" Gavin asked. "My apartment is tight quarters, but it's a hell of a lot better than the Dusty Rose."

"I'm sure we'll be fine."

Cash was a private person. The idea of staying with him—and it sounded like they'd be in separate parts of the house—wasn't as crazy as it'd seemed at first. She could observe the side of him he rarely showed in public. And that sort of closeness might lead to an intimate evening where he shared his secrets with her. Her neck grew hot again, prompting her to remind herself that intimacy in this case would not include more kissing. Or other…stuff.

She was here to do a job and that job didn't include a lengthy perusal of Cash's body—naked or otherwise. God, it really was hot in here. She fanned her face as her phone buzzed from inside her bag.

"Cash?" Gavin guessed as she checked her text messages.

"Yes," she said, her heart tapping out a hectic rhythm. She felt nineteen again. *A message from Cash Sutherland! Eee!*

But the text was merely an address. No *hi* or *drive safe* or even a smiley-face emoji. Disappointment took over where her excitement left off. It was just as well. There was nothing left between her and Cash but memories.

Six

Presley hung around in the VIP room and enjoyed appetizers with Hannah and Hallie while Will, Luke and Gavin stood in a manly huddle at the private VIP bar. So caught up in conversation with the Banks twins, she hadn't realized how late it was until she was hiding a yawn with one hand. Finally, at nearly midnight, she pulled up to Cash's house.

Well, she pulled up to *an iron gate in front of his* house.

"Seriously?" she asked no one. Except someone heard her.

"Door's unlocked, Pres," came Cash's deep, smooth voice through the box stationed outside the gate. She tried not to be aware of how sexy he sounded. Tried not to relive the searing kiss he'd placed on her lips earlier tonight. But here she was, thinking of both.

The iron bars swung aside and she drove in, a slightly cool breeze blowing her hair through her open window. She was exhausted from a long day of travel and socializing. So exhausted that it took her a minute to absorb what was in front of her.

Cash's house.

Cash's *enormous* house.

House wasn't even the right word. It was more like a mansion. Beaumont Bay was littered with them. The Bay marketed itself as a bustling, high-octane town that never slept, but clearly the people living there had to, and they chose to do so in luxury.

Her coworker Ray had written an article on celebrity houses a few years ago, right before she'd come to Tennessee to interview the Sutherlands about Elite Records. Curious, she'd searched online for photos of Cash's home. This had not been the house in the photo. He must have upgraded.

The sound of trickling water drew her attention as she stepped from her Jeep onto the cobblestone drive. A fountain, lined with thick greenery and vibrant flowers, was splashing into an in-ground pond. She peeked into the lit water and spotted several orange-and-white and black-speckled koi fish.

She still couldn't square Cash with all this luxury. He favored cowboy boots and black T-shirts. Though she couldn't say he was as approachable as he'd been when she'd gone to school with him, he was a true family guy. Fame didn't suit him, but he'd seemed to settle into the fancy vibe of this town just fine. Probably because he was from here, a fact she'd overlooked when they were in college. She'd let herself believe he belonged in Florida with her.

She rolled up the windows of her Jeep in case of rain, grabbed her suitcase on wheels and, out of habit, locked the doors. Probably unnecessary considering the large iron gates at the front, but whatever. Hopefully her room wasn't far from the front door. She was damned near ready to collapse.

As instructed, she depressed the button on the big antique brass handle and let herself inside. The second she set foot in the house, a voice echoed across the expansive foyer. A female one.

"You know how I feel about it," the woman said, her tone clipped. She had an accent. English, maybe?

"Yeah, and you know how *I* feel about it," Cash returned sternly.

"Well after going round and round for the last two hours, we're not apt to agree."

Cash's voice dropped into a seductive husk. "Since when has that stopped us from making this work?" Presley could hear the smile in his voice. And it sounded like a real one. A genuine, kind one. The way he'd talk to a girlfriend. The way he used to talk to her.

"You're so full of it. I'm out of here, handsome," the woman replied.

"C'mon, Rickie, don't leave. I have plenty of space here."

At his cajoling, the English woman let out a

laugh. Presley's stomach did a barrel roll. Rickie. His agent. Apparently, she was representing more than just his career.

How dare he kiss Presley in that elevator when he was attached to someone else? Her ire crept up, the rush of adrenaline waking her up. She could forgive his rudeness, his distance, but not cheating. That was unforgivable.

The soft scrape of clothing sounded like Cash and the woman were hugging. Presley braced herself for the smooching sure to follow, but the kissing sounds never came. What did come, as Presley stood in the foyer, her eyes squeezed closed, was a greeting from the woman that was much, much closer than before.

"You must be Presley."

Her eyes fluttered open to find the agent smiling at her. Rickie was older than Cash. Like, *thirty years* older. Her pale, ice-gray hair, cut into a long bob, was a beautiful fit with her bone structure.

"He told me you were staying here." Rickie shot out a hand and Presley shook it. She peered over the other woman's shoulder at Cash, who stood, arms folded, not the least bit concerned about being overheard. Not appearing the least bit guilty.

"I'm Cash's agent, Rickie Simmons. He's a complete bear, but I hope you'll go easy on him in the article." She cupped her mouth and stage-whispered, "Whatever you have to do to butter him up, love, feel free to do it."

"Rickie, for God's sake," Cash complained.

"You kids." She waved him off with a hand. "So

sensitive. I'm teasing, of course. Good night, you two. Don't stay up too late!"

She shut the door behind her and the cavernous space echoed with her retreat.

"She's the worst," Cash said, his smile teasing. He stepped forward and reached out a hand and because Presley was dazed and really very tired, she reached her hand out, too. He gave her palm a gentle squeeze and murmured, "I was going for the bag."

"Oh! Right. Sorry. I'm—it's been a long day. First the drive and then the concert and then I was caught up at the VIP room…" She stopped talking, figuring it was silly to give him details about the concert he'd performed or the room where they'd mingled in following.

"Don't sweat it. Follow me."

They walked through what very well could have been her dream kitchen if she'd ever bothered to dream up such an elaborate space. The gray granite countertops and rich brown wooden cabinets were high-end and gleaming. Textured stone flooring extended into a living room where a huge fireplace tracked up one wall to a high ceiling, and fat leather couches stood waiting for several guests to settle into their plush cushions. A staircase curved to a second floor, bisecting a hallway leading in both directions. The house was gorgeous and lush, manly yet stylish. A lot like its owner.

"Assuming you don't want a full tour right yet." He paused, one booted foot resting on the bottom step. His stance was casual and welcoming, definitely contrasting their interaction earlier.

She offered a head shake, too overwhelmed to say more. Today had been a lot to process already.

Upstairs they passed doors—a lot of them—and while her bedroom wasn't quite in its own "wing," it sat off by itself at the end of the hallway.

"How many guests do you usually entertain?" she asked as he wheeled her suitcase through the doorway.

"The band stays here sometimes, but this year they splurged for a houseboat on the water. They stay up late and party. I don't do that much anymore."

Much.

What'd it look like when he did, she wondered? Probably a lot like his mug shot, she answered herself. He was a crazy-famous bad-boy music star in a town of luxury and endless parties. Fifths of Jack Daniels, smoking pot and groupies must be commonplace for him. She frowned, hating picturing him dripping with faceless, nameless women.

"Rickie's a pill. Hope she didn't rankle you."

"I thought I walked in on a fight between you and your girlfriend," Presley blurted out. His agent was pretty, and it wasn't *that* far-fetched to think she and Cash had…*you know.*

His laugh was hearty. "God, no. Her wife would strangle me, for one. For the other, I'd never compromise our working relationship. You know how hard it is to find good representation?"

"No."

His smile held for a beat. She didn't know if it was her unexpected response to his rhetorical question, or if his smile was left over from the idea of him and Rickie dating, but either way Presley liked seeing it.

"Bathroom is attached." He pointed at the en suite.

She took her first look at his guest quarters, which could comfortably hold a family of four. And their dog. "Don't you have anything bigger?"

"Too audacious for you?" His grin was a little knee-weakening. It was hard to be this close to him and not remember what they used to do together. Hell, what they'd done mere hours ago.

He lifted the suitcase and set it on a king-size four-poster bed, adorned with several plum-and-cream-colored pillows resting on a floral quilt. She touched the stitching, unable to help herself. It was beautiful work.

"Real Southern charm, courtesy of Dana Sutherland," he said.

"Your mom sewed this?"

"She decorated this entire room. You didn't take me for a purple-and-flowers type, did you?"

She shook her head. "No, not really."

A rolltop desk stood between a pair of tall windows. Layered drapes matching the quilt hung on either side of them. She peered out the windows and down at the driveway at her Jeep, admiring the tall, manicured line of hedges she'd overlooked when she'd driven in.

"This place is—"

"Audacious. I know," he murmured, directly over her left shoulder.

She whirled around and her mouth was closer to his than she'd planned. Her mind immediately went to the elevator. The kiss. Her hands on his body, his hands on her waist. The way he'd pulled her close. She'd been more than happy to press her hardening nipples against his solid form…

She took a deliberate step away from him.

"When, um, did you get the tattoo?"

He blinked, and it was a relief when his intense gaze left her face. He rolled up his short sleeve and revealed the rest of the colorful guitar and music notes looping his biceps. "The night I won a Grammy."

"Are the notes from any song in particular?"

"The one and only."

"'Lightning,'" she guessed.

"I peaked too soon." He rolled his sleeve down.

"You have a long career ahead of you." She plopped down onto a stuffed chair next to the bed and tugged off one high-heeled shoe. With a groan she rubbed one aching foot. "Thank you. For letting me stay here. I know you didn't plan on housing me. I sure didn't plan on intruding."

"Come on, Pres. It's not an intrusion."

"Well, after—"

He held up a hand. "An apology is not necessary."

"An apology?" What was he talking about?

"I mean it. Don't worry about it."

"Why would I apologize?" Shoe in hand, she considered throwing it at his head.

"For getting carried away in the elevator," he said, his tone set to *duh*.

Her grip tightened on her shoe. Seriously, she was going to brain him with it.

"*I* got carried away," she repeated, exasperated.

"I know. But it's okay. Happens all the time."

He pulled his hands over his chest and for once she didn't admire the snug fit of his T-shirt sleeves at the biceps or the way the soft cotton molded to his pectorals. At least, she didn't notice as much as she'd noticed earlier.

"Everything you need should be in here," he continued. "Except the coffeepot, but I'm up bright and early so there'll probably be some for you when you come down. Night, Pres."

He shut the bedroom door behind him. She sat alone in the massive room, her shoe in her hand, and blinked dumbly at the door. She thought about the easy way he'd smiled at her, the calm way he'd joked with her and, finally, the outrageous way he'd accused *her* of attacking *him* in that elevator.

"Does he have amnesia?" she asked the empty room. He was delusional if he thought this was the end of that subject. After she'd had a good night's sleep, she'd pour herself one of those cups of coffee he promised and set the record straight about what had happened in that elevator.

For good.

Seven

Presley slept like the dead.

She woke up later than her usual seven o'clock, but after a day filled with travel and socializing—and kissing Cash Sutherland—it wasn't that surprising she'd slept in a few extra hours.

She couldn't bring herself to regret it. Dana Sutherland's homemade quilt was cozy, and spread over a mattress that might well have been crafted out of clouds. Pres woke well-rested and with a smile on her face, but once she was in the shower working mango body scrub down her legs, memories of last night returned, and with them came a frown.

Cash had said she didn't need to apologize for kissing him. She chuckled anew at his audacity. He'd *very obviously* been the one who'd initiated the kiss in the elevator. Not that she'd resisted, but that was hardly the point. The point was it'd happened, and it wasn't happening again.

Leaving her hair damp, since it was already eighty-two degrees outside and the sun would quickly dry it the rest of the way, she jogged downstairs.

Last night the house had been gargantuan and gorgeous. It still was, but the sun streaming in through the wide windows, offering a droolworthy view of the sparkling lake, made the house feel more inviting. It was still a mansion with a kick-ass kitchen, but at the same time it gave off cozy bed-and-breakfast vibes.

She lifted the coffeepot to find only a small puddle of the precious brew left in the carafe. Luckily, she didn't have to do water-to-coffee math since there was also a one-cup-coffee-pod situation on the corner of the counter.

Thank goodness.

Coffee brewed, she mentally reviewed the speech she was going to give Cash. Before she had a chance to set off and find him, music lifted on the air.

Guitar strums to be precise. The sound grew louder then quieter, like the notes were being tossed on the wind. She crossed from the kitchen to the attached living room and squinted at the sun-dappled water beyond the French doors. Her eyes tracked down to the beach and then back to the house before she spotted him. He was sitting on the wide steps of the deck, his back to her, his guitar resting on his lap.

She opened one of the doors and quietly closed it behind her, not wanting to interrupt. His smooth voice drew her in like a siren's song, the familiarity wending in her brain and tangling up in a memory she'd been sure she'd repressed.

"Will you play for me?" She'd been dating Cash Sutherland for almost two weeks. She'd seen him perform. She'd gone to a party with him. She'd stared at him shamelessly on the football field before he'd even known her name. And last night, she'd kissed him until she was breathless, simultaneously nervous, excited and finally disappointed when his hands failed to dip beneath the cups of her bra.

"What do you want me to play?" He strolled in from his kitchen, drying his hands on a dish towel. He didn't live in a dorm like she did. He had an honest-to-goodness apartment because, as she'd learned, his family had money. A lot of it. Good looks, musical talent and wealth seemed an unfair advantage over other guys, especially since Cash was also an amazing athlete.

Look at those guns. Yummy.

He lowered onto the couch next to her and she inhaled his spicy cologne. He lifted the guitar that was leaning against the wall and sent her a smile. At that second, she decided she was certifiably insane for holding on to her virginity.

It'd seemed like a good idea to be cautious when she'd started college—she'd heard horror story upon horror story from her girlfriends about how predatory college guys could be. And while she didn't think of Cash as "predatory" she did worry that once he slept with her he might realize he hadn't meant to court the chaste good girl. That he'd take her virginity and leave her behind, destroying her thoroughly.

Even so, she could think of almost nothing but shedding her clothes and being horizontal with him. Especially with his thick arms exposed, his deft fingers plucking the strings, and that low, sensual way he hummed in the back of his throat before he started singing... She was beginning to believe that the heartbreak would be worth the memories if the worst came to pass.

"Morning," Cash said now, head still bent over his guitar.

She snapped out of the memory, frustrated by her naïve former self. She'd gone back and forth over the years about whether she should have or shouldn't have given him her virginity. In the end, she hadn't, and had ended up heartbroken anyway. On good days she told herself she was glad she hadn't fallen any deeper for him, and on the bad ones she wondered if he wouldn't have left her if she had slept with him.

"I didn't want to interrupt." She folded her arms over her chest. "I always enjoyed hearing you play."

He peeked over his shoulder at her, one eye narrowed against the bright morning sunshine. The hand that had been strumming came to rest on the body of the guitar as she sat on the step next to him.

"You found coffee."

"Well, someone drained the pot so I had to be resourceful." She sipped from her mug.

"Well, *someone* slept so late that the batch I made would have burned if I hadn't drained it."

She turned her head to smile and found him smiling back at her. Utterly attractive and utterly distracting.

"Nice view you have here," she said, reaching for an excuse to stop looking at his rough yet handsome face. The water appeared deep blue thanks to the sun, and a boat trolled by in the distance.

"I like it. It's peaceful." He went back to strumming, his eyes on the water. She wondered if he knew he was doing it, or if the instrument was a part of him. Her eyes tracked to the tattoo on his upper arm and she figured that it *was* part of him, quite literally.

"I didn't kiss you yesterday, by the way." If she didn't say it now, she never would.

"Beg your pardon?"

"Last night you said I didn't have to apologize for kissing you."

"You don't."

A growl sounded in her throat and then her voice went an octave higher when she argued, "I refuse to apologize."

"So you enjoyed it," he concluded.

"You're impossible." She had to laugh, because if she answered truthfully she'd say she'd enjoyed it very much. What she hadn't enjoyed was the way he refused to acknowledge his part in it. "For the record, you were the one who kissed me."

"'For the record' is a very journalist thing to say," he muttered, sounding displeased.

She was aware he was changing the subject, but she let him. She hadn't made much headway, and frankly it was probably best not to talk about kissing him. Especially since she was trying not to think about kissing him again.

"Gavin told me you weren't a fan of journalists."

"Ever since I became famous, the press has been challenging. Since the DUI, they've been as charming as a school of barracuda." His fingers moved over the guitar strings and he sang, "And I wasn't expecting the likes of you."

He grinned. She rolled her eyes.

"Gavin also told me you'd say no if you knew I was coming."

"I would have."

That hurt. She'd had just about enough of this conversation. Whenever she was around him, he found a way to hurt her feelings.

"This was a bad idea." She was delusional to think that spending this much time with him wouldn't leave her raw and vulnerable. When she moved to stand he placed a hand on her bare knee.

"I'm glad you're here."

"You're *glad*?" That sounded like an overstatement. Gosh, it was hard to think when he was touching her. Thankfully, he pulled his hand away.

"Sure, why not?"

A million reasons why not. Like, she was his ex-girlfriend and he'd left her high and dry in Florida. Like she'd sneaked onto that elevator and he'd responded by kissing her senseless. And she must've been senseless; otherwise she wouldn't have slept in his house last night.

"You seemed upset with me yesterday," she said, unable to keep from steering the conversation back to them.

"Not at you. Clearly," he mumbled.

"So, you'll admit you kissed me?"

"You looked too damn cute not to kiss." His blue eyes burned straight through her as her heart pattered desperately against her rib cage. "But it won't happen again."

If it was possible to be thrilled and frustrated at the same time, she was experiencing that strange and yet-to-be-named emotion.

"That would be best." She took a sip of coffee and reminded herself that kissing Cash Sutherland...*again* would be the height of stupidity. She was staying in his house. He was speaking to her. She was halfway home. All she had to do was keep her wits about her a few days more. If he started talking about songwriting, maybe his guard would drop and he would casually admit the inspiration behind "Lightning". It was worth a shot. She cleared her throat and gave him a smile. "Do you practice every morning?"

"Lately, yeah. I'm writing." He pointed at a battered spiral notebook resting next to one of his thick thighs. "There are about five words on a page from this morning."

"Not going well?"

"It's going as well as it can go," he said. Cryptically.

"Can I help?"

His mouth slid into a half smile that was, like the rest of him, entirely too appealing. "You offering to be my muse?"

"I'm offering professional help."

"You mean like a therapist?"

"No, though you could benefit from one." She bumped her knee against his. He let out an easy laugh. He was so much less intense than he'd been yesterday.

"In case you haven't noticed, I'm a writer and words are kind of my thing."

"I noticed." The way his gaze locked on her implied he'd noticed more than just her profession.

A chill skated down her spine despite the warm summer sun. Him noticing her was only fair since she'd done nothing but notice him since she'd arrived.

"I like to write alone." He began strumming again, almost purposefully ignoring her. Just like that, he'd shut down. Smiling, friendly Cash was a memory.

"So do I. I'll be inside if you need me." She stood. He didn't try to stop her.

"The kitchen island has outlets if you want to work at the counter. Otherwise, there's an office upstairs. Doesn't get much use. I mostly work out here or in the studio downstairs."

"Thanks," she said, not meaning it.

At the door, she paused when he started singing "Lightning," the pull of his voice almost enough to make her linger and listen as he scratched out every heart-rending word. *Almost.*

Steeling her spine, she forced herself to walk inside.

Eight

The next morning Presley was downright chipper. The day was warm and sunny, the sky blue and clear. She practically skipped downstairs in her white gauzy cover-up, her bathing suit underneath.

After her run-in with Cash yesterday morning, she had retreated to the sanctuary of her laptop. The article about him was her priority, but the rest of her work hadn't magically stopped because she was here. She'd kept busy answering emails, writing blurbs and wrangling cute GIFs to post online celebrating a *Legally Blonde* remake. Thankfully, the assignments didn't require too much brainpower.

She and Cash had silently agreed on a truce and had reconvened by lunchtime. Will and Gavin stopped by to talk business around the same time Cash had opened the fridge in search of food.

Gavin had mentioned he was excited about a potential sponsorship for Cash, but Will's focus had been solely on the progress of the album.

Watching their interaction as an only child had been a little overwhelming. While her parents doted on occasion, they were in no way as involved in her life as Cash's family was involved in his. Though he seemed to take their presence in stride.

Cash and Will had then filed downstairs to the studio, where Cash practiced a new song. Presley had been invited to watch but she'd made an excuse about needing to work. Which was true, but still an excuse. His singing on the deck had caused a full-on flashback, and she wasn't anxious to experience another one of those.

Cash also had a way of making her defenses climb sky-high. Being defensive tempted her to argue about the past, which would derail her goal while she was here. She hadn't come here to argue with him about the past. What was done was done.

Or at least it should have been.

As the practice sesh stretched into evening, pizzas arrived for dinner. She and Gavin had eaten upstairs. She'd asked a few softball questions about Elite Records and Gavin's star client list, typing notes into her laptop in between bites of her dinner. Cash hadn't emerged from the recording studio. She'd seen Will for a few seconds when he grabbed one of the pizza boxes, but he'd taken it downstairs.

Once Gavin left, Presley had retired to her room. She'd dozed off, waking around midnight when she heard Cash open and shut his office door, which was near the guest room on her side of the house. By then she'd decided to enjoy her stay here at *Chez Sutherland*, and stop worrying so damn much.

As work vacations went, she could do far worse than a luxurious mansion perched on a lake, even if said mansion came outfitted with a surly musician.

That brought her to now, where she skipped to a stop in a kitchen. Cash stood at the countertop, his hair mussed, sleepily watching the coffeepot.

"Rough night?" she teased.

"Very funny," he replied, droll. "How'd you sleep?"

"Fine," she said, rather than tell him she'd heard him clattering around in the wee hours.

"Heading over to Elite in a bit if you want to come with." He sent a slow, thorough glance over her sunbathing attire. He still managed to make her skin sizzle with just a look. That was unfair. "You might want to change first."

She crossed one arm over her waist and bit down on her lip. The awareness permeating the air between them sure was inconvenient. "Are you sure you want me there?"

His head jerked on his neck, bringing his gaze to hers. "Why wouldn't I want you there?"

"Thought you liked to 'write alone,'" she repeated his words from yesterday.

"Write, yes, but I'll perform in front of you anytime, Pres."

The offer shouldn't sound nice, but it did. He was exhausting and she hadn't been here twenty-four hours. She was supposed to be wearing him down, not the other way around. "So you're recording today?"

"Yeah. Will and I eked out what we think is a workable song last night."

"You don't sound convinced."

He lifted his shoulders into a tight shrug. "Nothing feels right lately. There's usually a moment when everything clicks. When the words and the music come together. Sometimes that pours out at the beginning, other times not until the seventh or eighth time I lay down the track." His smile was almost sheepish. "That probably makes no sense."

"It does, actually. My articles don't come out great the first time, either. My boss, Delilah, says the magic is in the editing process."

"Do you agree?"

"Sometimes. Other times it's like you said, it pours out at the beginning."

He pulled two mugs from a cabinet and filled them with coffee. "Still take cream and sugar?"

"No sugar."

His eyebrows jumped like he hadn't expected that. He should have. People changed, and she'd changed a lot over the years.

He delivered her coffee with cream, leaving his black. His coffee hadn't changed. And maybe, she mused, neither had he. Maybe he was the same man capable of loving her and leaving her, the way he'd been on that long-ago rainy night.

Presley had changed from the gauzy white dress into a long, striped skirt, sandals and a white tank top. She looked good, but not as good as she had in a bright pink bikini that had been visible through the white sheer cover-up. If he closed his eyes, he could still picture it.

She'd pulled her hair into a high ponytail, her bright red locks glinting through the windows of his Bugatti on their drive over. She'd always been damn cute, but the cute he could handle. He didn't quite know what to make of her saucy, fiery attitude. She could turn it on when she needed to, that was for sure. She wasn't capitulating, didn't hesitate to tell him what she thought—or at least some of what she thought. He was sure there were plenty more thoughts bouncing around in her pretty head than what she'd shared with him so far.

They'd spent the better part of the morning at Elite Records. Cash had laid down a song he was calling "Fragile" and then he and his brother had gone over some of the other ideas for the album.

Will made a good sounding board. Not to mention he had a vested interest in Cash's album, specifically in the album going platinum. Success wasn't good only for Cash; it was good for his entire family. After college, success came at him like a tsunami, sweeping him up in the tide before he knew what happened. Some people had a slow and steady climb to the top. His was more like being shot out of a cannon.

He liked success for what it afforded him, so that he could do what he loved. The support of his fans gave him the freedom to write what he wanted, knowing they were along for the ride. After the DUI, it'd felt like that freedom had been taken from him. Like he was being corralled at every turn.

He'd rolled his eyes at his "bad boy" reputation at first, the moniker the result of desperate press grabbing for attention. Fans loved Cash, but they might have loved controversy even more. His reputation with women was far less scandalous than the gossip websites made it sound. Yes, he'd dated plenty, but he wasn't leaving a trail of broken hearts in his wake.

Though, he supposed Presley was the exception.

Since the mug shot, he'd been thrust into a different spotlight. "Bad influence" was a lot less charming than "bad boy." What pissed him off most was that he wasn't guilty of the crime he was currently paying penance for. Damned if he could prove it, though. The arresting officer hadn't changed a lick of his story since the night it'd happened, but Cash had been sober enough to notice the other man's shifty eyes.

Not that it mattered at this point. The damage had been done and had seriously messed with his head alongside his reputation. He'd been stuck on stupid for so many weeks, he wondered if he was capable of finishing this damn album.

Presley being in his immediate proximity wasn't

helping him focus. Especially when she looked as cute and carelessly sexy as she did while doing nothing but walking across a room. More than once he regretted never making love to her while he'd had the chance. Maybe if he had, he wouldn't be so damn curious about her now.

He closed his eyes and blew out a breath.

"Don't sweat it," Will told Cash now, evidently noticing his frustration. Thankfully Will didn't know why his brother was frustrated, or Cash would never live it down. "You'll get there."

Cash was prepared to work well into the evening, but he'd left Presley in Gavin's empty office too long already. He headed down the hall, the telltale clacking of keyboard keys falling silent when he rapped his knuckles on the door.

He let himself in and she looked up, her blue eyes wide.

Damn. Cute.

"You want to grab some lunch?" He glanced at the half-eaten candy bar at her elbow. "Or was that it?"

"The commercials were wrong. It didn't satisfy me at all."

They left the studio for downtown, passing by the boardwalk and a league of barely dressed men and women on the shoreline. The sky was as blue as it'd ever been, the sun almost blinding considering he'd been stuck in a windowless studio all morning.

Every building they passed, Presley read the sign aloud. A tattoo shop, coffee spot and, finally, the restaurant she decided she'd like to try. "How can you not have lunch at a place called Cheatin' Eats? It's positively *naughty*."

It was more than that. Cheatin' Eats belonged to Mags Dumond. Typically he was dead set against lining the woman's pockets, but he'd promised to let Presley pick so here they were. At least he knew he wouldn't run into Mags here. Like most of this town, she owned the place, but didn't participate in running it.

He requested a table outside and they sat. Presley, sunglasses tilted up, sunshine glinting off the lenses, let out a breezy sigh. "This sure beats being stuck in my office in Florida."

"You there a lot?"

"Almost exclusively. Hopefully I'll be doing more traveling in the near future." She smiled at him. "This article is sort of make-or-break. No pressure."

She opened her mouth to say something else, but it didn't come. Her jaw dropped as she watched a couple stroll by. She leaned over the table and whispered, "Oh my God. Is that...?"

"Asher Knight? Looks like him."

Her lashes fluttered. "I loved his band Knight Time. I hear they're recording another album. Do you think that's true? Do you think it'll have country music vibes? Is that why he's here?"

Cash couldn't help chuckling. "He wouldn't be the first rock star to cross over. I thought you were cool under pressure with celebrities. Pull yourself together, woman."

Her cheeks pinked. "I am. Usually. Everyone gets starstruck sometimes."

"You're not starstruck with me," he fished shamelessly. Hell, he'd been the one struck dumb. He'd been the one who'd kissed her before thinking it through. He could blame decades-old claustrophobia and proximity all he wanted, but deep down he knew why he'd done it.

He glanced at her lips. He'd just…wanted to.

The waiter arrived and they both ordered cheeseburgers. Pres opted for sweet potato fries while he went for the beer-battered onion rings.

"Do you eat here often?" she asked.

"Never." He sipped his iced tea.

"Is the food bad or something?"

"Not at all. Mags Dumond owns it."

"The First Lady of Beaumont Bay?"

"One and the same."

Her lips quirked. Mags's bulldozing personality was infamous 'round these parts.

"You should have told me. We could have eaten anywhere."

"Yeah, but you wanted to eat here." And he'd liked giving her what she wanted. He'd liked seeing that sparkle of excitement in her eye.

"The name is like her record label," Presley said, figuring it out. "I should have put that together."

"I can't forget. She asks constantly if I'm going to jump ship at Elite and record with her instead."

"Even though your own brother owns the studio?"

"Even though."

"That's…ostentatious."

"That's Mags."

Presley's pursed pink lips wrapped around her straw and she sucked down some water. That wasn't so much cute as it was hot. Made him remember kissing her. Made him think of doing other things with her. *And to her.* He forced his eyes away.

"Weren't you at one of Mags's parties the night of the DUI?"

He stiffened, caught off guard by her inquisitive tone. He should have expected that question. Presley, a reporter, was doing her job. "Yeah. Black-tie fundraiser."

"Fancy."

"Around here, fancy's commonplace." He nodded in the direction Asher Knight and his wife, Gloria, had gone. "That wasn't the only celebrity in town who doesn't live here full-time. People clamor to be added to her guest list."

"Including you and your brothers?"

"Nah, we're permanently on that list. She keeps her enemies close," he said, only half joking. "And so do we."

"We'll fix it," she said, sounding confident.

"My reputation?" He let out a humorless laugh. "Unless you can erase the media's memory, not sure you can fix a bogus DUI."

"Bogus? So you're innocent?" She lifted her water glass.

"I'd never make that claim." He sent her a cheeky smile. "It was late. I was tired."

"Maybe you should've been charged with driving while up past your bedtime instead."

He chuckled. She'd always been clever.

"Did you have a date that night?"

His smile vanished. He'd do well to remember they weren't old friends playing catch-up. She was here to write about his family—him in particular. A prospect he'd never be fully comfortable with. "No date."

"I imagine it'd be hard to date when everyone around you is speculating about your love life. Especially when you're writing an album. It's only natural to wonder about who influences the lyrics."

He sputtered into his iced tea and had to mop it from his shirt with a napkin. "Wrong pipe."

"Talking about exes does that."

So did his ex talking *to him* about his exes. For Cash, a private life was virtually nonexistent. But he hadn't expected Pres to bring up the one topic he'd refused to answer whenever it'd been broached by a member of the press. He wasn't sharing the inspiration behind "Lightning" with anyone. Especially her.

Their burgers were delivered. In between munching on a fry, she asked, "Is there someone special in your life right now?"

He lifted his sandwich. "You're nosy. Did anyone ever tell you that?"

"Everyone tells me that." She didn't take offense. Nor did she let up. "So, are you?"

"No. Are you?"

"I'm focusing on my career."

"Same," he said, then stuffed the burger in his mouth to keep from saying more.

The truth was he'd managed to live his life separate from the women he dated even while he'd dated them. They knew the score, honored the code, and he didn't have to worry about breaking another heart.

After breaking Pres's young heart, he'd consoled himself that at least they hadn't slept together. That would have made moving on harder, and he didn't only mean for her. He'd already been in neck-deep with her. Stripping her bare and taking her virginity would have made it damn near impossible to walk away from her, and by then he'd already made up his mind to leave.

Not sleeping with her was both the smartest thing he did back then—or didn't do, as it were—and also one of his biggest regrets. The other big one was selfishly dogging his own goals and leaving her in the wreckage. He'd been so focused on himself back then, on achieving success and stardom.

Presley, either too angry to speak to him or for her own self-preservation, hadn't reached out to him after he left. He hadn't reached out to her, either. When he'd heard she'd been in town two years ago talking to Gavin, he'd been pissed off. She'd sneaked back into town to talk to his family, never bothering to let Cash know about it. He'd blamed Gavin for the subterfuge, but it wasn't his brother's fault. No wonder Gav hadn't alerted Cash of her arrival this time. Cash hadn't exactly been gracious before.

What he'd never shared with anyone was why

her avoiding him had bothered him so much. Seeing him would have hurt her, and he guessed that
even years later, she hadn't been able to forgive him
for destroying her heart while prioritizing his goals.
Damned if he could blame her.

"Did you ever?" he asked. "Have someone special?"

She took a bite of her burger, proving she wasn't
a big fan of answering questions about her personal
life, either.

"Well?" he prompted. "Did you?"

"I've had a boyfriend or two since, you know, *us*."
She shrugged and he wondered if it was to downplay
her mentioning the "us" thing—the "them" thing.
He didn't make it a habit to rehash old relationships
either, which explained the awkwardness. "Nothing
as impressive as a famous sitcom actor like Heather
Bell or an award-winning singer like Carla Strouse."

He'd be damned if she didn't expertly steer the
conversation back to him and his celebrity exes.

"I was the only famous person you dated, huh?"
he asked, deflecting.

"You weren't famous when we dated. Only after
you left."

He didn't think she meant it as a jab, but he felt
the knife-slice all the same. Leaving her crying in
her bed hadn't been easy. It'd nearly gutted him.
Which was probably why he offered up a few details
without her having to ask. "Famous people date each
other because it's easy. We have the whole fishbowl
lifestyle in common."

"So you dated Carla and Heather out of convenience? No sparks?"

Sex, yes. Sparks, not so much. He hadn't felt "sparks" in years. Unless he counted a certain elevator ride with his lunch date.

"The women you've dated are drop-dead gorgeous. You would have made beautiful babies together." Presley sounded nonchalant but her eyes swam with another emotion. That same hurt he'd just been thinking about.

"The women I dated were nice enough, but there wasn't more than attraction to glue it together. And…off the record?"

She nodded, leaning forward a little in her seat.

"You're prettier than any of 'em."

Her lips pursed. "I thought you were going to say something serious."

"I am serious," he defended. But she didn't believe him. Maybe it'd be easier if she thought the years between them had erased every emotion they'd shared. As if every memory of her in his arms had gone up in smoke the moment he'd crossed the Tennessee border.

Thing was, it hadn't worked out that way. Cash had told her he'd left to pursue the dream absolutely eating him alive. That was true, but what he hadn't admitted was that committing to her would have cost him both his time and attention—two things he couldn't afford to give up while throwing everything he had at being a musician.

It was an ugly truth he still hadn't forgiven himself for. And if he couldn't forgive himself, he had little hope that Presley ever would.

Nine

Not again.

For the last two mornings, Cash had been writing in his studio rather than outside. Sometimes the change of scenery helped him create. Lately, he'd been chugging along and, while writing was not seamless, at least he'd found momentum.

Also for the last two mornings, he had stopped cold on his way to the coffeepot for a refill after becoming completely distracted by the vision on the other side of the French doors.

Presley Cole had taken to sunning herself on his deck.

She wasn't naked but damn near. Dark sunglasses were perched on her nose, her red hair aglow under the noonday sun. She was on her back on one of his oversize bath towels, her pink bikini bright against crisp white terry cloth.

Today her arms were at her sides, one knee up, the other leg closest to him stretched long and straight. Perky breasts rounded the incredibly sexy string bikini top. A long time ago he'd had his hands on those breasts. He'd had his *mouth* on them. He'd made her come while touching them.

He blinked hard and forced his thoughts to the present, something he'd done a lot lately. Having her here was like opening a time capsule, one he'd prefer stayed sealed and buried. It wasn't easy to come face-to-face with what he'd missed out on in the years since they'd lost contact. Having her here, knowing she was as single as he was and sleeping in his guest bedroom and sunbathing on his deck, made focusing on anything hard. And that wasn't the only thing that was hard.

He glanced down at his empty coffee mug. He'd originally come up for a refill. After lapsing into a brief fantasy involving Presley minus her bikini top and with his mouth on her, perhaps a cold drink would be a better idea. He pulled a jug of homemade sun tea from the fridge, hesitating briefly before grabbing two glasses.

For three mornings, he'd attempted to push thoughts of her aside. He'd tried to keep up a wall, distancing himself from her like he would any other reporter. Problem was, she wasn't any other reporter. This was Presley Cole, and she'd crumbled his wall now the same as she had years ago.

In other words, his tactics weren't working.

She wasn't leaving for a few more days, so he was going to have to find a better coping mechanism than pretending he didn't want her. Today, rather than avoid her, he'd try something new and dive in headfirst.

He strolled outside with the iced tea glasses in hand. Walking the other direction—as in *away* from her—would be smarter than inviting her to dinner and seducing her, but he planned on doing both anyway.

Whether she forgave him for leaving her all those years ago or not, he saw no reason why they couldn't satisfy their desire for each other in some sort of in-between realm. A kind of sexual purgatory, that would be more like a reprieve. Then he could stop fixating on what he could have done with her back then and just freaking do it already. The what-if scenarios had lingered in his head for too long. At this point, he'd be better off knowing what he was missing. Now to get her to believe that too.

"Thirsty?" He was parched now that he stood over her glistening body. Her belly was flat and bare, sweat dotting her skin thanks to the hot, midday sun. She was as tempting as if she was lying on a platter. Answering beads of perspiration dampened his upper lip.

"How'd you know?" She pushed her sunglasses on top of her head and sat up. She blinked blue eyes the color of the lake before taking her glass and folding her legs beneath her.

He sat on the freshly stained deck boards, close enough to smell the coconut-scented oil on her skin. God, he wanted a taste of her. Just once. Just so he could settle the debate in his head about how good she'd tasted back then. He'd had his lips on hers the other day and that had proven his memory for shit. Her kiss had been far more potent and consuming than any he remembered from their past. Or maybe he'd forced himself to downplay her potency, knowing he couldn't satisfy both his desire to leave and his desire to have her before he did.

"I love the heat. It's the one tolerable element of Florida," she said.

"There's only one?"

She shrugged one freckled shoulder. He wanted to trace those freckles with his fingertips, slip the bikini top off and follow the path of his touch with his tongue. He guzzled half of his drink and watched a boat zip by on the water instead. He wasn't stupid. Seducing Presley this time around required finesse.

"I love Florida but I'm tired of being there all the time. I've always wanted to travel. To see the world. Somehow the years passed and I haven't moved an inch. I thought I was on a journey up a mountain, but it ended up being more of a circular track. I looked up and realized I hadn't actually gone anywhere."

"You're here," he pointed out, a fact he hadn't been able to ignore.

"Yes. I am. I like this town. It's lush and beautiful. I can see why the rich and famous come here for leisure."

"It's home." It had been for his entire life. His parents had leaped on the real estate opportunities here, never expecting all four of their boys to go into the music industry instead.

"When I visited two years ago, I couldn't picture you here. I figured you must have changed, become a different sort of person who prefers luxury and the finer things in life."

"And now?" he couldn't help asking.

"Well, your house is luxurious, but you're…you. You love your family and songwriting and…" She bit her lip, seeming to think better of what she'd been about to say.

"And?" he prompted.

"It's corny."

"Honey, I write love songs for a living. Corny's my jam."

She blushed but held his gaze. The endearment, a byproduct of Southern charm, called up the memory of Presley's honey-sweet skin.

"You make what could be a very snooty town seem laidback." She sipped her tea before adding, "Comfortable."

So despite his attempts to be prickly, she saw right through him. He questioned the wisdom of seducing her after all, especially given how observant she was when it came to him.

Didn't change the fact that he wanted her. Badly. Lately, it'd been all he could think about, which was risky for him considering she was keen to ferret out his secrets. Letting her close could be disastrous for his career—and for another part of him he didn't want to examine too closely.

She straightened the center of her top and jostled those gorgeous breasts, and he told his second thoughts to go to hell. Some fires were worth the burn.

"Am I hogging your writing spot?" She sounded sincere. Like he'd come out here to reprimand her. She likely had no idea how she'd affected him this week, while she wore next to nothing or hell, even when she'd worn *something*. Her understated beauty had always been his weakness.

Frustrated, and not only sexually, he let her know exactly what he thought of her sunbathing in his "writing spot."

"Yes," he answered. "You're hogging my spot."

Her eyebrows flew up. He'd surprised her. He was about to surprise her more.

"I like it. I have liked it every day since you started coming out here. Wearing that tiny bathing suit, on your back, your hair spread around you like a fiery halo."

"Oh." Her mouth dropped open softly. He smiled. He'd been right. She had no idea how she tempted him.

"Do you want to go to dinner with me tonight?"

He wasn't sure if she'd say yes or hell no, but a jolt of satisfaction shot down his arms when he asked. He missed taking risks. He'd played it safe since becoming famous, recent bogus DUI aside.

He hadn't come this far to back off now. He was done resisting her.

"Sure," she answered, appearing way less affected than he was. Of course, she probably wasn't sitting here imagining licking him from head to toe the way he was imagining doing to her. "What's the occasion?"

"You have questions for your article I haven't answered. Figured we'd do it over dinner and get you out of this house. Into a nice dress. On the town."

All true, but not his main motivation for tonight.

Her pink lips pulled into a smirk he was dying to lean in and kiss. "How *nice* does this dress have to be?"

"Bord du Lac is jacket required. They have a coat check. A sommelier. I can't send you back to Tallahassee without experiencing the upper crust of Beaumont Bay."

"Well, who am I to turn down a fancy dinner with a famous musician?" Like before, she'd tried to sound nonchalant, but the sentiment didn't fly. He was too close to her to miss the excitement flickering in her eyes.

Eyes that dipped to his mouth and up again.

The glance was brief, but he'd noticed. Maybe she had been attempting to resist him after all. Trying to keep from fantasizing about *him*. There was a tantalizing thought.

She'd turned the elevator ride from hell into a slice of heaven the moment she'd kissed him back and pressed her body against his. If that happened now, he'd have a hard time not hiking her skirt up, pushing her back to the wall and begging her to take every inch of him.

It would be indecent. Inappropriate.

Fantastic.

"It's a date," he said, making sure there was no doubt in her mind what tonight was about. If she gave him a second chance to kiss her, he'd take that kiss as far as she'd allow. He let his eyes trail down her body before shaking his head gently. "Damn, Presley."

Then he stood and went back inside before he changed his mind about tonight and attempted to seduce her right now.

Presley had successfully collected Hannah Banks's phone number from Gavin. She'd told him she needed a woman's advice on where to shop for a nice dress for the restaurant she'd be going to with Cash tonight.

Gavin had tried to placate her with, "It's Beaumont Bay, not the Oscars. Wear a dress. Any dress," To which Presley had replied, "Strapless or sleeves? Do I need a wrap? Is the air-conditioning usually cranked or is there outdoor seating? What about shoes? Are the floors shined to a fine polish, in which case I should skip the spiked heel in favor of a wedge, or—?"

That's when he'd cut her off and shared Hannah's number.

When she'd called Hannah's number, however,

her twin sister, Hallie, had answered instead. It made sense given Hallie was Hannah's manager. Presley explained her predicament and was surprised when Hallie invited Presley to her apartment to "peruse" her closet. Presley hadn't wanted to be rude, so she accepted the offer, even though she doubted she'd find anything she liked from Hallie's neutral, conservative wardrobe. But she drove over there anyway, racking her brain for a way to politely decline when she didn't find what she was looking for.

Now, Presley stood in the closet of Hallie's first-floor apartment gawping at the clothes in front of her. On one side of the walk-in was what she'd expected: neutrals and black, demure hemlines and classic, timeless style.

On the other side hung the antithesis of "demure" and made her wonder if Hallie had a split personality. The clothes on the left were high-end, some with tags dangling from the sleeves. Some had sequins, others lace. Long formal dresses best suited for awards shows and shorter skirts perfect for a nightclub. They were in rainbow order, ranging from vivid reds and pinks to warm peaches and orange. Vibrant yellow to autumnal mustard to spring green, and sky blues fading into moody purples and plums. Beneath the gowns were rows of shoes in every color, size, shape and style.

"Wow," Presley muttered. What else was there to say?

"Hannah gives me the castoffs from her sponsorships. She receives tons of clothes from designers and companies who beg her to be photographed wearing them. She helps them sell a lot of clothes that way."

Presley stroked the skirt of an emerald green dress. The fabric was exquisite. "I can imagine." She frowned over her shoulder at Hallie, a copy of Hannah with her pert nose, warm hazel eyes and wide, sensual mouth. She wore a plain beige wrap dress and white sneakers, her blond hair in a braid down her back. Her style was understated, but she was every bit as beautiful as her sister. "You don't wear any of these?"

She shook her head and offered a small smile. When she did, a pair of dimples punctuated her cheeks.

"You have dimples." Presley hadn't noticed before. "Does Hannah?"

"Just me." Hallie blushed. "Dimples are a genetic defect. It makes sense that Hannah doesn't have them."

Presley wanted to hug Hallie and assure her there wasn't anything defective about her, but she didn't know the other woman well enough. She didn't want to make Hallie uncomfortable, but she couldn't keep from touching the other woman's arm in a show of support. "Most men would argue the defect thing. Dimples turn them into puddles. They melt at the sight of them."

"Really?" Hallie's smile lost some of the caution it held before. Presley wondered if there was a guy in particular who'd popped into the twin's head. She didn't have a chance to ask before Hallie went on to say, "Back to the task at hand. I may not look it, but I know how to dress for a nice dinner. I used to help Hannah before she hired a professional stylist."

Hallie slid a dress aside and then another, plucking down a red one and then a green one and taking turns holding them in front of Presley. This went on for another five minutes before Hallie decided they were done browsing.

"This one." Hallie's dimples reappeared as she pressed the hanger to Presley's front. "This is it. I'm sure of it."

Presley faced a tall mirror in the closet and tried to imagine herself in the gorgeous dress. Tried to imagine how Cash would react to seeing her wearing it. "It's not too much?"

"No way. Try it on. I can do minor alterations if needed. And please tell me you wear a size eight or eight-and-half shoe?"

"Eight," Presley answered.

"Perfect." Hallie bent to the shoe rack while Presley stepped into the adjoining bathroom and pulled on the very expensive, very finely made, very beautiful dress that Hallie had chosen.

As luck would have it, it fit like a glove.

So did the shoes.

Ten

Bord du Lac was jacket-required fancy, but there wasn't a tie requirement. Fine by Cash. He'd pulled on a dark pants and a jacket over an open-at-the-collar white button-down, threw on cowboy boots and called it a day. He didn't bother shaving since "scruff" was the look he preferred—and the look a poll favored according to a recent magazine article—and he did his usual hair routine, which was running his hands through it and letting it fall. A splash of cologne on his neck was the only fanciful part he bothered with, in case Presley leaned in for a whiff.

He stepped out of the master bedroom and jogged downstairs, expecting to wait for her for another ten or twenty or thirty minutes. He was surprised to find her standing at the kitchen counter, rummaging through a small sparkly handbag. She looked up when he reached the bottom step, where he was awestruck by the vision before him.

Her red hair was down, falling in big, bold waves around her deliciously bare shoulders. His eyes ate up her creamy skin on display, and there was a lot of it to enjoy. The dress was strapless, hugging her breasts and nipping in at the waist before flaring to allow for her luscious hips. He took in those long legs, capped by a pair of high-heeled shoes in the same slate-gray color of the dress.

She turned and the overhead lights caught the rhinestones—slate gray wasn't the only color on the dress. There were also icy-blue and almost-black bits, and the whole of it twinkled like the nighttime sky. When he finally managed to reroute his eyes to her face, her bubblegum pink mouth was parted innocently. Her thick, jet-black lashes weren't so innocent, closing down over blue eyes and causing parts of him to stir with interest.

Parts of him that wanted nothing more than to say *screw dinner*.

"I'm ready early." She sent one hand down the side of the dress. His gaze followed her hand hungrily. The dress stopped way before it should've—high on her thighs—and dipped low in the front, too, giving him a view of her cleavage.

Drawn in, he walked over until he was right next to her and could look down at her from his height.

With great effort he unstuck his tongue from the roof of his mouth. "You look incredible."

She tipped her chin, sending her hair falling down her back. The woman was sex in stilettos.

"I have a wrap in case it's cold in there. I wasn't sure." She fiddled with a piece of material next to her purse, almost absently, but she never took her eyes off him. "Cash?"

He didn't know why she said his name, but he was already on the move. His lips touched hers for a soft, brief kiss. So soft, it shouldn't have turned him on. So brief, he wanted to howl when it was over.

Feeling like a dope for rushing in, and yet not the least bit sorry for it, he smiled and moved away. "It's a sin to hide those shoulders, but bring the wrap."

He collected his keys and followed her through the foyer, pulling open the front door for her. By the time she folded into his car, he wasn't sure how he was going to successfully drive to Bord du Lac with his eyeballs glued to her legs.

He succeeded, but only because he'd trained his gaze on the windshield like his life depended on it. Distracted driving wasn't limited to cell phones and fiddling with the radio. His ex-girlfriend riding shotgun and crossing one silky leg over the other while wearing tall, spiked, bad-girl heels was enough to send him flying off an overpass.

Inside the restaurant, they were led to a private back corner reserved for famous folks. Before Cash's fame peaked, he'd been mildly amused by the idea of famous people needing a "safe haven" for dining, but now he understood it. A visit to a nice restaurant could quickly become a nuisance. The few dates he'd been on in public were documented by every diner, whether they were a member of the press or not.

Even now, as he walked with Presley through Bord du Lac, he felt cell phone cameras pointing in their direction. He hoped he wasn't making her the topic of a tawdry headline. "Don't look now," he murmured in her ear, "but we're being watched."

She scanned the dining room before whispering up at him, "I can handle it."

Which reminded him that this was not the Presley from a decade ago. She hadn't curled into a ball and withered away. She'd followed her dreams just like he'd hoped, gaining newfound confidence thanks to her achievements.

Their table was hidden behind decorative privacy panels, the booth backs high and ensuring they wouldn't be bothered. Their nook was cozy, but big enough to accommodate multiple plates and glasses. The paneling extended on two sides with an opening wide enough for the waiter to stand and take their order or pour the wine, which he did before giving them privacy.

"This is very elegant." Presley lifted a balloon-shaped glass and sipped the red wine. He did the same. She'd already moved her silverware so that the ends lined up on the napkin, touched the edge of the candleholder to see if it was able to be repositioned and drummed her fingers along the leather-bound menu at her right elbow. All signs that she was nervous, and doing her damnedest to pretend she wasn't. "I'm glad Hallie loaned me this dress."

"*I'm* glad Hallie loaned you that dress." His words came out on a growl. "You couldn't look more beautiful if you tried, Pres."

She surprised him by smirking. "Is that why *you* kissed *me*? *Again?*"

He deserved that. "Yeah, but if you don't want me to kiss you again, say the word."

It was a test, but she didn't say no. Instead she relinquished her wineglass before leaning back in her seat to study him. "What's your favorite Cash Sutherland song?"

Back on the clock.

His guard climbed, a habit he'd honed after learning the press went for the jugular. He'd like to believe Presley wasn't after blood. Still, he gave her a canned answer.

"My songs are like my babies. I couldn't pick a favorite child and neither could I pick a favorite song. They're all a part of me."

"That's cute." She tipped her head in disbelief. She was the cute one. "Now the truth. Favorite song. And why."

When he didn't answer, she added, "I'm not publishing a recycled Cash Sutherland article a hundred other writers have penned. I want the real you. The public wants to know the man behind the guitar is a genuine person."

Genuine. He liked that word. He wanted to live up to it. Aspired to reach it. Fame, while it allowed him to share his most personal feelings on stage, could also be inauthentic. It forced him to smile when he didn't feel like smiling, or perform when he'd rather be sacked out in front of the television. His fans thought they knew him, but they only knew a version of him. *Genuine is the summit of the mountain I'm climbing.*

"One sec." He pulled his cell phone out of his pocket and pecked those words into the notes app on his cell phone. He wasn't sure if he'd stumbled across lyrics to a new song or if it was a flash of an idea that wouldn't pan out. Either way, he couldn't risk losing it.

"Did you suddenly have a burst of inspiration?"

He considered the sweet, beautiful redhead across from him and thought, *hell yeah I'm inspired.* "Hit me out of nowhere but I couldn't ignore it."

The same could be said of her.

"'Lightning,'" he answered belatedly, and this time, honestly. "'Lightning' is my favorite Cash Sutherland song. I wrote it and rewrote it for years. I agonized over every word and practiced it until my fingers bled. I can sing it in my sleep. I can perform it and call up the way it felt to put those words to music for the first time. It's part of me, that song— that's the truth. Indelible. Inseparable. Undeniable."

Her features softened. The facade of cunning and eager journalist fell away, leaving just Presley. As if his honesty pierced the armor she hadn't known she'd worn.

"Pure," she said. "Your love for that song. That

must be why it resonates. Why whenever you perform it, it's like you're singing a memory."

She didn't know it, but she had him dead to rights. He was singing a memory all right. A memory of a certain red-haired, blue-eyed and, yes, *pure* girl he'd been halfway head over heels for.

Presley Cole. The one who got away.

Or, more accurately, the one he'd left behind.

He couldn't let her go home to the Sunshine State without them finally sharing the one thing they hadn't. He couldn't live with another decade of regret. While he believed the lyrics of "Lightning," which said it never struck twice, he would accept a few distant flashes in its place.

A night or two with Presley in his arms would give him an idea of what he'd missed out on years ago, satisfying the hollow ache that had resided in the center of his chest since. And maybe, her walking away from him this time would heal the hurt from what he'd done to her. Win, win.

She was bold, smart. Driven. She could hold her own anywhere, and with anyone. He desperately wanted to find out if that would be true in his bedroom.

Throughout dinner she continued quizzing him. About his music and the new album. What it was like to work with his brothers closely. If there was any competition between them for Biggest Alpha Male—her words. That question made him laugh out loud. No, they hadn't competed. They were each in their own corner of this crazy industry and content to share the spotlight.

Halfway through dinner, his guard dropped, which was less about the wine and more because of the company. Presley was still easy to talk to. The word *genuine* bounced around his head again, a few disjointed chords and notes bouncing with it. He wouldn't dare take his attention from her to write them down.

"How'd Will deal with the duet between you and Hannah Banks?" Presley swallowed the end of her wine and set the glass aside. "You and his wife-to-be essentially sang a love song to each other. Did it make him jealous?"

"No." Again, Cash laughed. "Hannah and Will are inseparable. He had nothing to worry about, and he knew it. As wonderful as she is, she's not my type."

"Famous and beautiful isn't your type?" She tapped her chin in faux consideration. "Your exes Heather and Carla might disagree."

"What about my ex-girlfriend from college?" he asked, his voice low. "Would she disagree?"

"I'm neither of those things."

"You are a *famous* journalist—"

"Hardly."

"—and the most beautiful woman I've ever laid eyes on."

Her delicate throat moved as she swallowed. She might not believe him, but he was telling the truth.

As beautiful as the women he'd been photographed with were, none of them were Presley.

"Cash Sutherland," she scolded, her tone playful, "are you trying to seduce me?"

"Yeah," he answered. "I am." That wiped the smile off her face. "And if you want to end this night in my bed, your arms and legs wrapped around me, a light sheen of sweat coating our bodies after we've wrung each other out in the best way imaginable, I suggest you let me."

Eleven

Presley didn't make it two steps into Cash's house before her purse was taken from her hands, her back was pressed against the closed front door and her mouth was covered with his.

She reacted the way any red-blooded woman would, by wrapping her arms around his neck and accepting his tongue into her mouth. The kiss had the urgency of the one in the elevator, but none of the haste. As he proved a moment later when his hand tightened at her lower back and he slowed down.

Way down.

His lips moved over hers in a soft, rhythmic way before they moved to her neck and *oh yes*, that was so much better. She arched her back and closed her eyes, lost in the sensation of his hands on her waist and the scruff of his jaw scraping the sensitive skin of her throat.

"You smell good." His voice was a low rumble. She'd always loved that deep baritone. It made her feel safe and it made her feel sexy, especially right before he nibbled on her earlobe.

When he backed away, her hair clung to his cheek. She liked seeing it there, the red strands mingling with his short, dark facial hair. His eyelids were low, his full mouth damp. He was so hot it was criminal.

"I see you decided to let me seduce you." A cocky grin slid across his mouth and she couldn't help smiling back at him. She hooked a finger into his belt loop and tugged him closer. His hips bumped hers, the sturdy ridge of his erection evident and tempting.

"What base are we stoppin' at tonight, Pres?" he murmured as his hands climbed her torso. He paused on her rib cage, just shy of cupping her breasts.

"Home run, cowboy," she breathed, trying to sound more confident than she felt. She felt a lot of other things. Jittery and excited. Impatient and willing.

After he'd left her in Florida, she'd cried her heart out. She'd also kicked her own rear end around campus for saving her precious virginity instead of sleeping with him while she could have. A year later she'd gifted her V-card to a guy in her Advanced Writing 202 class and had been as underwhelmed as she'd expected. He was nice enough, but she hadn't cared about him the way she'd cared about Cash.

The out-of-place memory made her sad and Cash, who was close enough to see straight through to her soul, noticed. His eyes flashed with concern and his mouth pulled into a loose frown.

No way would she let the past ruin this moment. "I'm not letting you escape this time," she said and then she kissed him hard enough that he'd forget what he saw.

It worked. The next words out of his mouth were, "Climb your sweet ass up the stairs and go to my room."

Liking his bossy side way too much, she turned and scurried for the stairs, her borrowed heels clicking along the way to the top. He caught her easily, linking their hands and leading her to his room.

She looked down at their arms, his deeply tanned skin and thick, calloused fingers looped with her smaller, paler fingers.

What are you doing?

Years ago, he'd broken her heart. It was big and it was unresolved. She'd sworn she wouldn't allow herself to be towed in by his magnetism when she began this assignment. So why wasn't she saying good-night instead of following him to his room?

Because.

She'd missed out on him once. She wouldn't miss out again.

What happened tonight would be a gift she gave her past self. And her present self. Her future self would have to learn to live without him, but she'd done it once. She could do it again.

At the entrance to his bedroom, he paused, leaned on the doorframe and gripped her hips with his palms. Those palms slid up her dress until they reached her breasts, but this time, he held them and drew his thumbs over her nipples. Without a bra, they leaped to attention. Then he moved those rough-feeling hands over her beaded dress and around, undoing the zipper at the back. When the front sagged, he tugged her top down and exposed her, his eyes going black as his widening pupils ate up the caramel brown of his irises.

She'd always loved when he touched her bare breasts. Her nipples were sensitive and currently shooting a zillion electrical charges straight to the apex of her thighs. Her breathing sped up and her fists clenched helplessly at his button-down shirt.

"Some things haven't changed. I know what you like."

Proving it, he dipped his head and took her nipple on his tongue. Slowly, he circled the tender bud as her eyes rolled back in ecstasy. Her hands relocated to his head, where she gave his thick hair a tug. He gently bit and then soothed her with his tongue.

After a few breathless moments of bliss, he backed her into the dark room, his mouth never leaving her breast. Then she was in the air, being tossed onto the bed. He climbed over top of her, his dark head lowering to her other breast, his finger plucking the nipple he'd rendered both damp and turgid.

Her hips rose and fell, mimicking what she wanted most. Cash seemed content to make her wait.

Finally, he guided his hand up her skirt, fisted her lacy underwear and rolled them down her legs. There was a frustrating moment where they became tangled with her shoes, which he insisted she keep on. Since he insisted while sliding his fingers up her inner thigh, she decided not to argue.

He stroked into her and, wet and ready, she easily accepted his finger. His tongue went back to work on her breast, sucking and pulling while his thumb joined the action, stroking her clit. She jolted and felt his smile against her skin. He knew what she liked, all right.

They hadn't had sex years ago, but he'd made it his personal mission to find a way around her rules. He'd found all the loopholes—and had managed to gift her the best orgasms of her life. She'd given herself several since, sometimes imagining his fingers between her legs, his mouth on her breast, but those imaginings paled in comparison with the real Cash Sutherland.

"Come for my fingers and I'll give you my mouth," he murmured against her nipple as she shook in his arms.

He continued his sensual assault and not long after she orgasmed as he'd commanded. The release was long and easy and freaking *fantastic*.

"Good girl," she heard him say and then vaguely became aware of him unzipping her dress the rest of the way, his hand at her back. "Arms around my neck, sweetheart. I have more kissing to do, only lower this time."

"Cash, you don't h-have to," she stammered, overwhelmed by what he was suggesting. He'd never gone down on her. And now, with a fresh Cash-induced orgasm lighting her bloodstream, she wasn't sure she could handle more.

"*Have to* has nothing to do with it." On his knees in front of her, he unbuttoned his shirt and pulled it off his shoulders. He'd stayed in shape over the years, filling out with muscle. The width suited him, the dark hair over his pectorals unashamedly masculine.

He'd been good-looking then. He was hotter than hell now.

Not only was his chest deliciously defined, so were his abs. She wouldn't mind exploring every hill and valley on his torso. A perfect innie belly button sat just above a trail of dark hair that disappeared into his pants. Behind his fly, his cock gave a peppy jerk and she squeezed her knees together. Then she nearly hyperventilated when he undid his belt and drew down his zipper.

"You're not making this easy on me."

"Looks pretty hard, actually," she said with a grin.

He gave her an admonishing glare as he stood and pulled off his clothes. He returned to the bed, still wearing black boxer briefs.

She shoved his chest with her high heel. "Those, too. Take them off."

He grabbed her ankle, pulled her leg to one side, took a long-enough-to-make-her-squirm gander at her naked body and then said, "And if I don't?"

"Don't make me come up there," she warned.

He laughed and any residual nerves faded away with it. To her delight, he stood again and shoved his fingers into the sides of those briefs, pushing them down his legs. His erection was on display, hard and glistening at the tip. She bit down on her lip. She was done being patient.

"Let's have sex. Don't worry about that other part." She nodded to encourage his agreement but he didn't agree. Not at all.

Grabbing both her ankles, he gently spread her legs and wedged his shoulders between her thighs. He looked good there. Really good. Her heart pattered out a desperate rhythm.

"Haven't you ever had anyone do this for you?" he asked, his eyes on her most private part, his thumb stroking her folds.

"Cash," she gasped. She licked her lips, her nerves returning. "It's okay, really."

She lost his touch and when she looked down at him this time, he was frowning. "Seriously?"

"I—it's not a big deal. I just, it's not something I enjoy?" She didn't mean to ask, but she'd asked. Over the years she'd convinced herself she wasn't missing out, but with Cash poised over her, preparing to deliver a tongue lashing that would be her first—and probably the best—she was positive she'd enjoy it.

His smile widened, a feral glint in his eye. "Damn, I'm excited. Here I've been thinking you experienced everything without me and I'm the first one who will—"

"Don't say it." The words were rushed out, and he obeyed her request in the best way imaginable. His tongue slicked over her center and a long moan escaped her throat. That was... That felt very nice. Incredible. *Indescribable.*

He cupped her ass and yanked her closer to his face, and then reached behind his head to pull off her shoes and toss them on the floor. "Second thought, you might impale me given you've yet to experience this."

"Safety first," she murmured. This time when he laughed it reverberated down her legs since he'd already set his mouth to her.

He toyed with her at first, delivering light, even strokes before picking up the pace and then slowing down again. Meanwhile she fisted the bedsheets helplessly, her hips lifting and rising to meet each stroke. When he homed in on one particular spot, her next exhalation was no more than a feathery rasp.

"Hang on tight. Here we go," he advised, and before she had a chance to tighten her grip on the sheets, he picked up the pace. Her hips rose to meet his thrusts, her heels scraping down his back, and in no time at all, she came on a cry. Her entire body hummed, the electric current from earlier still flowing through her veins.

He eased up, allowing her to enjoy the release.

Without his shoulders for support, her legs collapsed uselessly to one side. In fact, her entire body felt boneless. Sparks danced along the surface of her skin and entire cosmos burst behind her eyelids.

He left her briefly, but by the time he returned to bed his smug smile was locked in place.

"That," he said, lazily stroking his fingers up her arm, "was worth the fucking wait."

She laughed, but it was wheezy. She blamed the orgasm. It'd been a wringing one. She'd thought his hand was nice? His tongue should be bronzed.

"Guess I enjoy that after all." She faced him.

"Guess so." He flicked on the nightstand lamp and pulled open a drawer.

Her eyes on the foil packet, her breaths tightened.

"You're sure—" he started but she snatched the condom from his hand. No way she was going to say no to him.

"Get your ass in here," she demanded.

"Look who got bossy."

"You ain't seen nothing yet." She tore the condom open with her teeth, her hands shaking—her entire body shaking. When he climbed over top of her, she reached for him.

He helped her roll on the condom, which shouldn't have been sexy but somehow, with him, it was. Once it was in place, he moved her hand with his over his sheathed cock and down to the crisp hair encircling it. Up once more. Down once more. Her eyes turned up to his and what she saw there nearly stopped her cold.

Cash Sutherland. In the flesh. Several inches of him about to be joined with her for the first time. She'd convinced herself tonight was just sex but already she questioned if he could ever be "just" anything to her.

She shut her eyes against the thought. His lips kissed her nose before he said, "Presley. Look at me."

She fluttered her lashes, taking in his handsome face, his thick arms bracketing her. He appeared golden in the lamplight, a beautiful fallen angel.

"You good?" he asked.

"So good," she answered.

Then she reached up and cuffed his neck and pulled his mouth to hers. At the same time, he tilted his hips, entering her that first amazing, agonizingly perfect inch.

Twelve

He eased into Presley's sweet, giving body slowly, which was an exquisite form of torture.

There was no need to ease—she was wet and ready for him—but he didn't want to rush. He finally had her, had her approval, and had been the first man to give her an orgasm with his tongue on her clit. That alone was enough to make him blow.

So, by the time he'd eased in to the hilt, he'd had to breathe low and slow and remind himself he was a grown man who could hold out longer than a few pathetic minutes.

Presley wasn't helping in that endeavor.

She stroked his hair with her fingers, rocking her hips against his in a rhythm that was both gentle and deep. He wedged his teeth together when she touched his chest. Now she was murmuring words like "you're so hot, you feel good, I like your mouth the most," and he had to pause to issue a warning.

"Pres," he grunted as the pressure in his balls built to a dangerous level, "honey, you have to stop talking dirty or I'm going to lose it."

Her eyebrows rose. "I'm talking dirty?"

"Yes. And I like it. Way too much."

Upon hearing that, his vixen crossed her ankles at his thighs and arched her back. Her nipples were alert and begging for a kiss. He delivered one to each of them before she started again.

"I had no idea how big you were," she purred into his ear. "You used to be able to make me orgasm with your mouth on my breasts, but now that I know how good you are between my legs, I'm going to demand that from now on."

"Presley."

"Seriously. So *big*."

"Dammit," he begged.

"Don't stop."

Like he could? His hips pistoned between hers, desperate to find the release he'd sought since he entered her.

"Huge, actually," she breathed.

"Honey, shut up." He stamped a kiss onto her mouth.

"Not on your life." A flicker of challenge lit her eyes. "Tell me, what else can you do with your— *oh!*"

Her startled "oh!" was because he'd decided to

teach her a lesson, lifting her leg and hooking her knee over his elbow. He tilted his hips and drove deep, loving watching her blue eyes darken to navy.

He might be at her mercy, but he wanted her to know she was also at his.

"Yeah, 'oh,'" he teased. Her eyebrows scrunched, the whimper she released a melody he'd not soon forget. "You first, then it's my turn."

"I…already…had a turn," she breathed, with effort, given he hadn't stopped moving.

"You had two turns. This makes three." He seated himself again and her face contorted in a pleasure-pain expression. She was close. And, thank God, she went over after he doled out one more stroke.

He let go of her leg and propped himself on his elbows. Her arms lazily looped his neck and then she continued murmuring about how sexy he was and how hot he was and how big he was. This time he didn't stop her.

He found his own release shortly after hers, finishing on a growl, his face in her neck, his nose buried in her hair. His breath was shallow. His mind blessedly blank.

He surfaced after who knew how long, the sweat from their bodies cooling on their skin. That was when she turned her head and kissed his cheek, giving him so much sweet he could hardly stand it. Too much sweet after what they'd done. But that was Presley. She was sweet. Even when she was naked and talking dirty.

Before he could let that thought take root, she

murmured, "Wow" into his ear and for some reason that hit him and he laughed.

Hard.

She joined him, her shoulders bouncing beneath him, which was when he became aware he was crushing her into the mattress. He pushed up, slipped free of her tight hold and rolled to his back. Hand on his chest, he pulled in a deep breath.

"You wore me out, wildcat."

"I'm not a wildcat."

He rolled off the bed and went to the bathroom, calling over his shoulder, "Dirty talker, then."

Her chiming laughter followed.

When he returned to his bed, he found her sitting up, her breasts hidden behind his gray sheets, her sparkly dress in hand. He plucked the garment from her and tossed it onto the chair by the window.

"Got somewhere to be?"

Her hair was untamed after she'd rolled around on it for the last hour. And here he didn't think she could look any hotter than she had sunbathing on the dock. He was wrong. She looked hottest after she'd been sexed up, down and sideways and was wrapped in his bedsheets.

Mine.

He tried to shove out the thought when it came but he didn't succeed. Instead, it curled up in his chest and made itself cozy. Presley had been his once. It'd been a long time ago, and she'd been waiting to gift him exclusively what she'd given him just now.

That Wayne Gretzky quote about missing 100

percent of the shots you didn't take felt really damn true. He hadn't taken a shot with her and now knew what he'd missed.

But that didn't mean he would allow fantastic sex to distract him from finishing his album. Nor would he allow her to be distracted from what she'd come here to do. Long ago, they couldn't have slept together without becoming deeply entangled. Now that was not the case. They could—and they would— walk away intact. Even if the sex was so good it should be illegal.

"I was going to take my borrowed shoes and dress and go back to my room," she answered. "Did you expect me to sleep in here with you?"

And there it was. The line he hadn't thought to draw but, obviously, he needed to draw it. He eased back on the bed, shoved a pillow behind his back and curled her into his side. Arranging the blankets over both of them, he leaned over and kissed her wild hair, smiling against it when he thought about the tangles she'd have to comb out later. He hoped she thought of why they were there when she did.

"We should talk about that, yeah?" He felt her stiffen in his arms. "I want you here, Pres. In my bed. Naked in my arms. I want you on my dock, driving me crazy in your tiny pink bikini. But we should be clear about what this is…and what it's not."

She shifted and looked up at him, her blue eyes wide and innocent, her lips pursed gently. "What it's not."

"Yeah, honey," he continued, gentler than before. "What it's not."

"You mean…" She licked those pink lips and rested a hand tenderly on his chest. "You mean you aren't going to make an honest woman out of me now that we had sex?"

Cash's face broadcast myriad emotions. They ranged from regret to nervousness to confusion and finally to what she could only describe as "oh, shit."

Much as she was enjoying this, she let him off the hook with a laugh. Holding the sheet over her chest, she sat up. "I'm kidding! Cash, honestly."

His confused expression held a moment longer than it should have. "I knew that."

"I'm not the girl you left at Florida State. I grew up too, you know. I learned how the world worked."

She still cared about him, but she didn't expect a marriage proposal just because they'd slept together. She had a life separate from his. And she knew better than to fall for him this time around. He was a famed heartbreaker, and she didn't care to relive that experience.

"That was fun," she continued. "I had a great time. You had a great time. I'm looking forward to doing it again if you're up for it."

"If *I'm* up for it?" He let out a disbelieving chuff. That was better. She couldn't have him looking at her like she was precious, or who knows what mixed messages her heart would receive.

"You were the one begging me to stop talking dirty to you."

"I was not begging."

"Please, Presley, please stop talking dirty before I lose my mind!" she totally misquoted. Then she was dissolving in laughter, Cash having dug his fingers into her sides with the single-minded intent of tickling her to death. She squealed and then gasped for breath before managing a strangled apology.

When he finally let up, the sheet had fallen to her waist and her breasts were exposed. His leg rested heavy on one of hers and his erection was nudging her hip.

"You're different," she said, and didn't miss when he bristled. "Less bitter than when you left school. Happier, but somehow sadder at the same time."

His eyebrows closed over his nose in warning. She ignored that, too.

"Your family's success is important to you." She ruffled his hair away from his forehead, smoothing his furrowed brow with the tips of her fingers. "Have they always been? Did you accept that football scholarship to Florida State to make your parents happy?"

His jaw tightened. A muscle jumped in his cheek. She pressed on, curious.

"Are you writing this album for you, or are you doing it to bolster the success of Elite Records? I imagine it'd be a lot harder to be inspired if you are only trying to help the record company. Unlike your first album that birthed 'Lightning,' which came straight from the heart."

A thundercloud swept over his face. He no longer looked confused or nervous, but angry. "You in my bed gives you access to my body, not my personal life."

She flinched, but he kept going.

"You want to interview me, Ms. Cole, make an appointment."

"Cash—"

"Best you sleep in your own room after all."

She watched through narrowed eyelids as the stone wall formed around him. He stared at her calmly, not taking back a single sharp word he'd said.

"Fine." She hustled out of bed and collected her clothes and shoes. "We both got what we needed tonight anyway. We can talk more tomorrow if *your schedule* allows. How's ten in the morning work for you?"

A dab of regret washed over his features. "Wait—"

"Good night."

She wasn't waiting for whatever explanation he was going to offer. She was irritated with herself for letting him affect her this much. She should have shrugged off his grouchiness and left with her dignity intact.

Well, screw that. She could still leave with her dignity intact.

The couture dress wadded against her chest and strappy shoes dangling from her fingertips, she marched naked down the long hallway, her hair billowing behind her. She hoped he was watching her strut away from him. She hoped he was missing her body pressed against his. She hoped he was regretting that they weren't halfway into round two.

She shut her bedroom door, threw her clothes on the chair and climbed into the shower.

She was wrong. He hadn't changed. He was the same guy who, given half a chance, would shut down and send her away.

And even though she knew she'd crawl back into his bed again to experience more of what she'd had tonight, she was properly armored up this time.

Hopefully her heart knew better than to allow fanciful ideas about how he'd changed to take over like weeds in a garden bed.

Thirteen

Cash rapped on the guest bedroom door the next morning aware of two things. One, Presley was nowhere near waking up since it was before seven o'clock, and two, he'd been a dick last night and that required an apology.

He'd realized that last bit the moment she'd strolled away from him down the hallway, her bare, heart-shaped ass wiggling.

He'd had no idea how to make up for his temper or overreaction at the time, so he'd sat on it. By the time she'd closed her bedroom door—she didn't slam it, which was somehow worse—he'd muttered to himself about being an idiot and proceeded to lay staring at the ceiling trying to think of a way to make it up to her.

The answer had hit him about an hour ago. He'd been biding his time waiting to go to her room, but he couldn't wait any longer.

"Pres," he called, along with another knock.

Her sleepy, slightly grouchy voice sounded through the door a second later. "Go away."

He shouldn't, but he smiled. "C'mon. I have coffee."

Silence. Then, "The coffee I'll take."

"Well, you have to answer the door, honey, because my hands are full." He waited for what felt like a full minute before the door opened a crack. She appeared in the gap all bright blue eyes, a mess of red hair and an FSU T-shirt that'd seen better days. It wasn't his, but he'd had one like it when he'd gone to school with her.

She couldn't look any sexier if she tried, but he sure as hell couldn't open with that.

"Mornin'." He held up his hands—one of them holding the handles of two coffee mugs and the other wrapped around the neck of his guitar. "The rest of my gift is forthcoming. Can I come in or do I have to serenade you from the hallway?"

He'd been kidding, but she looked as if she might make him stand there while she glared at him through the crack. Luckily, she pulled the door wider, shameless about wearing nothing but a blue pair of panties beneath her T-shirt. Sexy. *Damn.* She did it for him. Even in a threadbare T-shirt and cotton underpants.

He settled the mugs on the high dresser and then handed her one. "Creamed, like you like it."

She mumbled incoherently and traipsed back to bed, jamming her legs under the covers, her back propped against the headboard. Her eyes closed as she took the first sip of coffee, a small moan communicating her gratitude. Another thing he'd learned about her years ago: if you show up early, show up with coffee.

He left his own mug and walked to the bed. She braced, but he kept coming until he'd lowered on to the side of the bed, his hip nudging her leg.

"This is called the apology song." He cleared his throat. Hummed for effect. Then he strummed a few chords and sang.

Dear Presley.
This is my apology.
I didn't mean to be so mean.
I didn't mean to be so much me.
Dear Presley.
I brought coffee.
And I'll do it gleefully.
Until you forgive me.
Will you forgive me?
I hope you forgive me.
I'm so sorry, Presley.

He hummed at the end, set his fingers to the strings and waited. He didn't have to wait long. Her lips curved up at one corner and she didn't waste any time taking him to task.

"Gleefully?" she repeated.

"Yeah. You should feel special since I don't do *glee*."

Her small laugh faded fast. For good reason. He couldn't expect to be out of the doghouse with a hasty, questionably funny song.

"Last night was—"

"Don't." She shook her head.

"I'm gonna," he informed her. She sucked in a breath that she let out in a huff and he continued. "Last night was good, Pres. Better than good. I wasn't prepared for…how good."

Meaning: the blast from the past that was Presley Cole had carried with it a truckload of memories.

"And because I wasn't prepared, I wasn't ready to deal with the crap that came up. Including you talking about those days again. And how I deal with my family. My defenses climbed sky-high and I blew it big-time. Laid in my bed and swore and stared at the ceiling long after watching you walk away."

"You did blow it," she murmured after a beat.

"I know." He rested his arm on his guitar. "Hope you don't regret it, though."

"I don't." She lifted her chin.

He could have guessed. She was strong. Strong enough to deal with the fit he'd pitched.

"I pried, though, and I shouldn't have. Insatiable curiosity is one of my traits. Not a great one."

She had that backward. He was the insatiable one when it came to her. "You didn't do anything wrong. I was just…being me," he finished lamely. He thought he'd be able to ignore their past, but when she'd mentioned "Lightning," he realized that was an impossibility.

He strummed the strings on his guitar and clumsily sang, "Come with me to a Fourth of July party. On Friday, Friday. Yeah, on Friday."

She raised her eyebrows. "For real?"

"For real." He continued strumming nothing in particular. "There's a party at Mags's mansion before the fireworks. After, we'll take the boat out, watch them light up the lake."

Will had called to ask if he'd like to join, along with Hannah, Hallie and Gavin on his boat, but Cash had declined. Then Luke had asked if Cash wanted to join him on his boat, and Cash had declined that invite, too. Reason being, he wanted to show Presley the lake and the fireworks and, if he could get her to forgive him, he preferred to be alone with her on his own boat.

He hadn't told his brothers that part.

He kept strumming. "The party will be a pain but after, you can change out of your formalwear. We'll have the boat to ourselves. Fireworks overhead."

"Formalwear?"

"Formalwear. Mags," he explained, which was the entire explanation.

"I love fireworks."

"I know." He stopped playing. Her eyes went to his hands on the guitar.

"I liked the part where you admitted you were mean."

"Figured you might."

"The coffee was a nice touch."

"Figured you'd think so."

"I don't want to fight with you while I'm here." She sighed. "But I'd like to keep doing what we were doing. If you're willing."

His mouth dried out. He'd hoped she'd accept his apology. Hoped he could convince her to attend the party with him. And yeah, he'd hoped he could have sex with her again. Eventually. He hadn't expected to be propositioned, which she did next.

"Are you? Willing?" She set her coffee mug on the nightstand.

"Now?" This was too good to be true.

"Now."

He wasted no time setting his guitar on the chair by the window and then yanked the blankets off her lap.

"With you, Pres, I'm always willing." He kissed her and she tasted like coffee. "This shirt." He feathered his fingertips beneath the hem and touched her bare stomach. "It's hot."

"You're crazy." She laughed.

He was. And his not being able to stay away from her was proof. He didn't care what she thought about him, just so long as she accepted him in her bed.

She did, and he spent the next hour and a half doling out part two of his apology.

Friday arrived. Presley tore the tags off the little black dress she'd purchased. It was short and classy, but also comfortable. She paired it with black high heels, also new, and packed a small bag like Cash had suggested. The bag contained her swimsuit, beach towel, a pair of shorts and a T-shirt. He assured her the water would be warm enough to dip into if she wanted to do so, and if she didn't want to do so while naked, to bring a suit. She didn't plan on climbing into the water, but she would rather be prepared. When it came to Cash, she'd surprised herself a few times already. She simply hadn't expected to enjoy him quite as much as she had. Lately, every time she was around him, *naked* was exactly how she'd ended up.

After he'd serenaded her in her room two days ago, they'd had another round and a half of fantastic sex. They didn't argue when they were done either, which was a nice change of pace. What followed had been a "normal" day, and he'd encouraged her to ask the questions she'd asked the night before. She did, tentatively, but he'd answered without much fuss.

Yesterday they'd sat on the dock and wrote. Cash, guitar in his lap, humming and strumming and occasionally jotting down words into a spiral-bound notebook that had seen better days. There were paper shreds stuck in a badly bent coil and she'd teased him, asking if that was the same notebook from when he went to FSU. That'd earned her a low laugh and a kiss, which she returned without argument.

Tonight was the formal affair at Mags Dumond's house, and would include her first boat ride since she'd arrived. She was ready for a night off, but acutely aware that tonight wasn't a night "off" at all. Her article was coming along, but she still needed some key information so she could end it with a bang.

As luck would have it, Hannah Banks and Cash Sutherland wouldn't be country music's only superstars in attendance. A source had confided that Carla Strouse would be there—as in Cash's ex. That source was Hallie, who hadn't a clue what Presley was up to and if Pres had her way, never would. Alas, when she published her article, everyone would know that she'd been seeking the truth to the inspiration behind Cash's hit song. She hoped Hallie and her sister, Hannah, Cash and the rest of the Sutherlands could forgive her for it someday.

"Slip out of those shoes," Cash said as she came downstairs.

She looked down at her black high heels. "Why?"

"We're taking the boat to the party. It'll be easier for you to navigate the docks without three-inch heels." By the time he finished talking, he was standing in front of her and smiling. "Four inches," he corrected, moving her hair away from her face to tuck it behind her ear. "Like you this tall."

"Thanks."

He kissed her. She lingered. When he released her lips, brushing her jaw with his thumb, she somewhat dazedly slipped out of her shoes and into the flip-flops she'd stowed in her bag.

On his deluxe pontoon boat—which was the fanciest pontoon she'd ever set foot on—she sat on one of the cream-colored vinyl seats and admired the shine glinting off every surface. How did he keep it this pristine?

He drove slowly since there were several boats dotting the water and they were in a "no wake" zone. The wind was at a minimum, so she wouldn't have to fix her hair when they arrived at Mags Dumond's mansion.

They passed other giant houses on the water, some towering with multiple balconies, others low and sprawling, partially hidden by thick, green-leaved trees.

"Come drive," Cash invited, holding out a hand.

"Really?"

"I'm insured."

"You're hilarious." She gave him a playful slap on the arm as he pulled her onto his lap. She took the wheel, and he moved her other hand to the throttle, murmuring instructions into her ear. Those instructions turned into praise for how good she smelled and then advanced to kisses on the side of her neck. By the time she closed her eyes, he teasingly reminded her she was going to wreck them into the rocks.

A short while later they arrived at Mags's lakefront mansion and docked in one of the few available spots left. She carried her shoes in one hand, leaving her boat gear on the pontoon, and walked barefoot up the dock. By the time they reached the walkway cutting through a grass-covered hill, her jaw was on the ground. She toed on her shoes, holding on to

Cash for purchase, while watching many, *many* well-dressed people file into the massive house.

"Let's get this over with." His tone was hilariously bored. As if the fanciest, most well-attended party in town was nothing more than a nuisance.

Her stomach jumped as she thought about speaking to Cash's ex-girlfriend. Tonight might be the night Presley found out if Carla was the woman fueling the sentiment behind his hit song.

Presley told herself she was simply satisfying her own curiosity, but that was a lie. She would have to write about what she learned tonight. Uncovering secrets was part of her job—Delilah had made that clear. And uncovering one this big would not only win her the contest at work, but also catapult her career *and* make her travel dreams come true.

She'd share what was in the article with Cash before she published it, though. She wasn't a monster. But she *would* publish it. And if he couldn't understand the reasons behind why she needed to, then he'd never understood her at all.

Fourteen

Presley was underdressed.

Who threw a Fourth of July party that was a suit-and-tie affair? Mags, apparently. Cash didn't care about dress code. He was dressed country cool in black jeans, cowboy boots and a black button-down shirt with bold, stitched embellishments on the chest. The women at the party were dressed grander in gowns or pantsuits bedazzled with glittering rhinestones or sequins or a combination of both.

Only when she saw Hallie did Presley let out a breath of relief. The other woman looked chic and professional in a sophisticated black pantsuit with a sash tied at the middle. Her high-heeled shoes were not as tall as Presley's, but enough to lift her so that the wide legs of her suit didn't brush the marble floors.

"I'm underdressed," Presley confessed instead of saying hello.

"No, you're not." Hallie smiled. "You look amazing. Hey, Cash."

"Hey, Hal. Seen my brothers?"

"I came with Will and Hannah, so yes. Luke popped in, but I don't know where he ran off to."

Presley searched the well-dressed crowd, spotting an incredibly famous country singer who had aged really, *really* well. "And Gavin?"

"Gavin?" Hallie squeaked, a blush stealing her cheeks. "I—uh, why would I know where Gavin is?" She sucked down an inch of her wine.

Well. That was an interesting reaction. Presley folded her arms over her chest and studied Hallie carefully, having the distinct impression that the blonde was hyperaware of Gavin's whereabouts while pretending not to be. "Why would you know where Gavin is, indeed?"

Cash picked up on none of this, his eyes traveling the room.

"If you need to mingle, I'm good here," Presley told him.

"Yeah?"

"Yeah."

He gave her a soft smile, followed by a softer kiss, and then let her go. He walked across the room, but not before promising, "Be back."

"Are you two," Hallie started, moving closer to

Presley to whisper the rest of her question, "back together?"

"No. Yes. Sort of." Presley winced. "I'm not sure I can have this conversation without a glass of wine."

"That can be arranged."

Hallie was not only beautiful and kind, she was also good company. Each with their own glass of champagne, they mingled among the famous, Hallie introducing Presley and making a smooth getaway so they weren't trapped in any conversation for too long.

Knowing Presley wanted to meet and speak with Carla Strouse, Hallie was sure to include the famous singer in their rounds. After an introduction, the twin excused herself and left Presley and Carla alone. Presley felt a ping of guilt that she hadn't been forthcoming about why she wanted to meet Carla, but she couldn't very well blurt out that she was going to grill Cash's ex about "Lightning," now, could she?

Hallie had found Carla Strouse on one of Mags Dumond's many balconies. This one was on the second floor and less populated than the patio below, where guests had spilled out into the yard and were littering the beach, as well.

"Anyway, enough of my gushing. I'm sure you're tired of me standing here reciting all the reasons I adore you," Presley said with a chuckle. That was the truth. She had always loved Carla's music. Gushing came naturally. "I assume at these parties it's gauche to morph into a fangirl."

"Please." Carla, both pretty and friendly, rolled her eyes. "I nearly *died* when I spotted Louise Hatton here. *Louise Hatton*, the woman who inspired me to sing when I was six years old! We're all fangirls deep down."

Carla, with her short, layered hair, full mouth and twinkling green-blue eyes, was more beautiful in person than she was on stage, which was quite the feat. She was also really freaking nice. Presley didn't know the reason for Carla and Cash's breakup, and she couldn't imagine one, either. They were both famous, attractive. They'd looked good together, too. There was no shortage of flattering photos of them online.

"You're here with Cash, right?" Carla brushed her hand along the shiny silver dress fitted to her lithe body.

"I am." Presley drank the rest of her champagne in a rush. She wondered if Carla was sizing her up and comparing. There was no comparison, really. Carla was a glowing beacon of perfection whereas Presley was, well, *not*. "We went to college together."

"In Florida." Carla's light eyebrows lifted.

Presley wondered how much Cash had shared with the other woman about those days. A petty part of her wanted to trumpet that she'd been with Cash first, but she hadn't technically been with him first, had she? She'd been with him only a few nights ago. Knowing that Carla had also been with him made Presley feel more than a little self-conscious.

"He's wonderful, isn't he? I mean, he's complicated. He is a man," Carla added with a delicate snort. "But he's great."

"He's, uh, he's all of those things." Before she lost her nerve, or her dinner, Presley decided to get to the point. "I've always thought you were the one, you know?"

She let the bait dangle.

Carla cocked her head, smiled quizzically and then bit. "'The one'?"

"Yeah. The woman he wrote 'Lightning' about. You two made a cozy couple. And you were together, what, eighteen months?"

"On and off." Carla's smile faded.

"Oh." Presley hadn't uncovered that nugget during her online research. "I just assumed… I didn't ask him about you, or anything. He doesn't talk about his past."

"Believe me, I know. He never told me details about anyone he dated before me."

"Really?" Presley was both surprised and unsurprised. Cash wasn't exactly an open book, but she'd expected him to be tight-lipped with her, *the reporter*. He hadn't shared his past with the woman he'd dated for a year and a half? Carla and Cash must not have been as close as the press had everyone believing. The words *on and off* suggested distance.

"Oh, to be the woman who inspired 'Lightning'…" Carla's smile didn't seem forced, but amused. "I wish he'd felt a fraction for me of what he sings about in that song. Whoever she is, she's a lucky girl."

"Indeed." Presley nodded tightly. One starlet down, one to go. Too bad Heather wasn't also in attendance at the party tonight. The actress lived on the West Coast. She and Cash had met while Heather was filming a movie in Nashville. Presley wondered if Heather and Cash were also "on and off" in the six or so months while they dated.

Presley and Carla moved on to tamer topics, talking fashion and hors d'oeuvres and music. Carla introduced her boyfriend, also her producer, who seemed like a decent guy. Cash meandered over and met Carla's boyfriend too, shaking the other man's hand and politely kissing Carla on the cheek. No longing glances were exchanged, no stiff, nervous smiles, either. Presley was beginning to believe what Carla had said about the nature of her relationship with Cash.

It was oddly relieving to know that during the brief time Presley shared Cash's bed, he wasn't having any lingering feelings for the likes of the beautiful, famous, likable Carla Strouse.

They returned to the bar and Cash handed Presley another glass of champagne. He ordered a Coke with lime, hold the Jack Daniels, for himself.

"Staying sober for the press?" she teased.

"I have to drive the boat." He bent and whispered into her ear, "And talk you into doing a host of bad-girl things on that boat." Now he was grinning and she understood why. He wasn't going to have to try hard to talk her into anything. "I have to be at the top of my game if I hope to…"

His words trailed off, his attention elsewhere. His arm at her back stiffened. "Get ready."

"For what?"

But then Mags Dumond slithered over to stand in front of them and Presley knew exactly *what*. The First Lady of Beaumont Bay had finally made her way to them.

Mags had to be around seventy, but her smooth skin betrayed her age. Her plastic surgeon was good. The woman looked every year of fifty, but not much older than that.

"Well," Mags drawled, the tassels on her ice-blue gown shimmering under chandelier light. The dress was weighed down with beads and rhinestones and should have made Mags look gaudy. Instead it only made her look *wealthy*. She was a woman who knew herself, knew her power in this town and reigned like the queen she believed herself to be. "Look who decided to grace us with his presence."

"Mags," Cash said through clenched teeth.

The woman turned to Presley. Her smile didn't budge, her pearlescent teeth practically aglow. "Mags Dumond. Most people around here know me as—"

"The First Lady of Beaumont Bay," Presley finished, offering a hand.

Mags's eyes narrowed. "Why, yes." She moved her martini from one hand to the other. When Presley took the other woman's hand, cool metal pressed her fingers from Mags's many chunky diamond rings, not one of them understated.

"Did you know—" Mags released Presley's hand "—Cash refuses to record at my studio? Even after a storm knocked Elite Records to the ground. I'm all for loyalty but that's just silly."

"Elite Records wasn't on the ground," Cash muttered, the flash in his dark eyes a warning Mags ignored.

"Close enough." Mags guffawed. "You're Presley Cole, aren't you? You're interviewing our boy for your hometown paper or whatever."

"Viral Pop is far from a hometown paper," Presley defended. "They have eighteen locations all over the globe, and a reach of over 100 million." Presley realized belatedly she'd stepped into the same snare as Cash. This woman was good.

"Huh. Who knew?" Mags shrugged with her mouth. "Well, I'll leave you two to…whatever it is you're doing. Anyway, Cash, even in the wake of your DUI and subsequent PR nightmare, my offer stands. Cheating Hearts Studio is not petty. Are you sure your brothers have your back no matter what?" She made a show of peering down at Cash's drink. "I hope there's no alcohol in that glass."

Cash's nostrils flared. If he hadn't been sucking in a breath through those nostrils, Presley would have sworn rigor mortis had set in. His arm at her lower back was positively rigid.

"I'm staying with Elite." He emitted a low exhalation that was a borderline growl, followed by,

"Mags. Always a pleasure," before excusing himself and leading Presley in the opposite direction.

"The pleasure was mine!" Mags called after them, loud enough to be heard over the entire party. Forget the storm that smashed into Beaumont Bay a few months ago, Mags was a force of nature with twice the wallop.

Cash steered them to the bar, set his Coke down and instructed, "Jack Daniels, rocks." Then to Presley he promised, "I can still drive the boat."

Once he'd taken a hearty sip of his drink and they'd moved to a less populated room in Mags's mansion, they walked out onto a small landing. Presley rested her forearms on the railing and looked down at the guests milling around below. She could feel that Cash had something to say, so she gazed up at the stars and waited for him to come around to it.

"She doesn't give up," he finally said. "She's been pressuring me for years. Went as far as offering me a movie role with one of her director friends in Hollywood. She doesn't care about my success. She wants the clout. Wants to be tied to every big name in the business. She went after Hannah the same way a few months ago. Nearly broke up Will and Hannah in the process. There's nothing magnanimous about what Mags does. Not ever."

Presley had zero doubts that Mags was the complete opposite of magnanimous after their brief meeting.

"That woman could drive the soberest man to drink," he muttered.

"Why do you guys come to these things?"

"You met a lot of people tonight. Famous people."

She had.

"Relationships are forged at these parties. Friendships made. Mags is the price of admission, and everyone is willing to pay. When Cheating Hearts was the only recording studio in the Bay, Mags was… Well, she was never *nice*, but she wasn't as villainous. When she had competition, she got worse."

"So on the one hand Elite Records makes connections at these events, but on the other they are forced to play by Mags's rules."

"Lest we suffer her wrath." He sipped his drink.

Presley blinked, a lightbulb of an epiphany flipping on in her head. "Literally, in your case."

Cash frowned, not following her train of thought.

"At that last party. You said she approached you to record with her?"

"Yeah."

"And you said no."

"I said 'hell no,' but close enough."

Presley touched his forearm. "And it was Mags who goaded you into one more drink when you were about to leave."

"She's persistent."

"That checkpoint, the questionable reading on the Breathalyzer. Could that have been part of her 'wrath'?"

His frown deepened, his eyes unfocused like he was thinking back to the night in question. "Earl."

"Earl?"

"The officer who pulled me over. They've been seen in town together lately." Cash's lip curled. *"Romantically."*

"Maybe he did her a favor. He set you up for her. That way she could approach you, claim to overlook your bad reputation and represent you anyway. Knowing you wouldn't want to harm Elite Records." It wasn't so far-fetched to believe. Mags would do anything to stay on top. "I can blow this wide open. My article can be your saving grace. I can demand a public apology for you. I can—"

He pressed his finger to her lips before shaking his head. "Let it lie, Pres. It's done."

"It's not done. It's an outrage."

"Past is past. No sense in dredging it up." He tipped her chin and she tried not to look into his eyes, tried not to see clear through to the sentiment behind it, and how it reflected her own need to dredge up the past. To find out who had inspired him to write the most heart-rending lyrics she'd ever heard in her life. To slay that mystical beast Closure, no matter what it cost her in the short-term.

"I have an album to focus on," he continued. "Elite Records is primed for a comeback. Write about that. No good can come of stirring the pot."

"But your mug shot," she tried.

"What's done's done." His tone communicated

he was also done having this conversation. "You ready to leave? It's almost time for the fireworks."

Heat shimmered in his eyes. She guessed he didn't mean only the fireworks in the sky. He meant the ones that would happen once he set his lips to hers.

Fifteen

Cash anchored the boat away from a fleet of other boats volleying for the best spot to watch the show. The fireworks hadn't started yet, so most of the noises bouncing off the water were the hoots and hollers and whistles of partiers on the lake.

The sky was dark. The crickets were singing and winged bugs large and small bounced off the lights on the front of the boat. That left Presley and Cash in the semidark, but she could still see nearly every inch of the boat's interior, which meant so could anyone else.

"Guess I won't be changing clothes since I have an audience," she told her captain.

"You sure about that?" He moved her to the side and pulled open a small compartment on the side of the dashboard. Up popped a privacy panel that stood taller than him and was twice as wide. The lightweight fabric was pale in the moonlight and billowed gently in the breeze. He opened a gap in the fabric and gestured. "Your changing room, miss."

She eyed the ample private space created by the fabric, "Okay, that was impressive."

"I aim to please." His hands on her hips, he followed her in and promised she was about to be more impressed. His lips hit hers and he unzipped her dress.

"How," she asked between kisses, "are we supposed to maneuver *this*?"

A whistling sound streaked up high, and because the fabric panels were open at the top, she watched as a colorful explosion burst overhead.

"We'll maneuver just fine," he assured her.

She returned his grin and began thumbing open the buttons of his shirt. He kicked off his jeans and she let her dress drop.

"I don't know what to hold on to." She scanned the tight, hot and getting hotter space.

"Hold on to me."

There was a pause as she considered her inability to hold on to him at one point in time. She pushed the thought aside as he shoved his boxers off his legs. She was going to give in to the magic of this moment. And, like a magician, he made her bra and thong disappear.

He wrapped her arms around his neck and then palmed her ass and lifted her. The tip of his erection nudged her center and she gasped. She was wet and ready for him after only a few kisses.

"You're like a drug, Cash Sutherland," she whispered against his mouth. "You should come with a warning label."

"Speaking of, I should probably grab a condom." He kissed her swiftly. "But I don't want one."

"I don't want one, either." She stuck out her bottom lip. "I'm—I can't get pregnant since I'm on the pill. So…"

She was nose to nose with him so she didn't miss the moment his gaze darkened with lust. *"Presley."*

"If it's safe. Are you? Safe?"

"Yeah, baby, in the way you mean. Totally safe."

She didn't think too hard about what other ways he wasn't safe. He was the bad boy of country music, after all. "Safe" didn't describe him.

He didn't give her a chance to overthink before he slipped past her folds and erased her mind.

"That's nice," she breathed, hugging his neck.

"Fucking fantastic," he agreed, lifting her off him before dropping her down. His arms shook with effort as he made love to her standing. She held on as he'd requested, her fingers in his hair and her truncated breaths in his ear. Sweat slicked her chest and she glided against his torso each and every time he slid into her body.

"Do you…want to…put me down?" She didn't want that. He was in deep, felt too good. She was ready to explode from pleasure.

"Never. Touch yourself, Presley. Help me out."

She untangled one of her arms and wedged her fingers between their bodies. After a few tender strokes from her own fingers and a few more thrusts from Cash, she found her release.

Her moan vanished under the sound of another firework explosion, the faint smell of smoke tickling her nostrils. She fought for her breath as he found his own release. He groaned into her ear, a deep, appreciative guttural sound lost under yet another firework going off overhead.

"I'm heavy. I can feel you shaking." The tremble in his arms and legs was apparent.

"That's not why I'm shaking," he muttered before capturing her lips in a consuming kiss. "You make me weak, Pres."

Boy, could she relate. She had the will of a wet paper bag around him. Tenderly, she unhooked her legs from his waist. He slipped free, making sure she was steady on her feet before letting her go. But he didn't leave right away. He bent his head and rested his lips against her neck, his arms holding her tight.

Being naked on his boat under the fireworks should have led to naughty, kinky sex. The kind of sex they'd just had was far more intimate. In the small, overheated space with his breath on her neck and his hands on her body, she came to an unpleasant realization. Somehow, even though she'd tried to stop it, Cash had burrowed past her defenses. He'd buried himself in her body, but he hadn't stopped there. He kept going until he'd wedged himself into her heart.

Yeah, baby, in the way you mean. Totally safe.

She trusted he wouldn't impregnate her or put her in any physical danger, but if she allowed herself to fall for him… Well, there wasn't anything safe about that, was there?

"Grand finale." He kissed her neck again as cracks, pops and whistles dominated the night sky.

"Thought we did that already," she joked, not feeling like joking at all. Not with the complicated emotions clogging her chest.

"You're amazing. Completely amazing." His top half vanished out of the privacy panel. He returned with a pair of board shorts and stuffed his legs into them. Then he stepped out, leaving her to pull herself together.

In more ways than one.

She cleaned up with a beach towel, tied on her bikini top and tugged on a pair of shorts followed by a T-shirt. Her arms shook, a warning that the mistake she'd made was bigger than forgoing prophylactics. Her chest felt too full. She missed him already and he was standing right outside the privacy panel.

She heard motors rev to life as boats left in search of another party opportunity. She emerged and Cash folded the fabric dressing room back into the dashboard before cramming his party clothes into a bag.

"Now where do we go?" She felt jittery, anxious to return to his house. Maybe then she could relax. Or at least retreat to her room.

"Nowhere." He lay on his back on the wide sunbathing bench on the back of the boat. "Come here."

She couldn't say no to him, which was most of her problem. She crawled onto the platform and tucked herself against his side.

"Best fireworks ever, don't you agree?" he murmured.

She inhaled the fragrant chemical smell of spent fireworks. "Incredible."

"Agree." His lips were close to her ear.

When she turned her head, she caught him watching her. She was propelled back to her dorm room, his bulky body taking up most of her twin-size bed, his eyes on hers while she apologized for making him wait to have sex with her. He'd always said the same thing.

You're worth the wait.

"You were worth the wait, too, Cash."

He knew exactly what she meant. His hand cupped her neck and then he was kissing her again. A boat blazed by and some guy shouted, "Get a room!"

He grinned against her lips, not letting the interruption ruin the moment.

They watched the sky in silence for a minute until she said, "I had a great time at the party. Despite Mags being horrible."

His low laugh was relaxed and easy. Quite a departure from his demeanor at the party earlier. She was feeling the equally relaxed. She could slip into a deep sleep while bobbing on the water with naught but his arm supporting her head.

"Carla is nice."

"She's a good person." He gave her a quick squeeze. "But she's no *you*."

Presley wanted to argue with the compliment, especially since she was planning on finding out his secret and exposing it to the world.

"I wish you'd let me help you with Mags," she tried again, unable to stop herself. "She deserves to be called out. You deserve to be happy."

He *was* happy.

Right now, with Presley in his arms, he was happier than he'd been in a long time. And because that light, easy feeling was a rarity for him, he didn't want to talk about his DUI or Carla, and he especially didn't want to talk about Mags Dumond.

"I don't want to talk about the past," he said. "You're here. I'm here. Let's talk about that."

She drew in an unsteady breath. "Okay."

After months of trying to control the media—impossible—and monitoring his every facial reaction and posting carefully online—annoying—he was more than ready to let the past go. Easier to do when it came to Mags or Carla. Letting go of Presley was proving harder.

"You should stay a while longer." He blurted out what he'd been thinking for most of the evening.

"S-stay?"

"Yeah. Another week, at least."

He'd told himself he was blowing off steam with her, that they'd have their fill and move on. But they'd had sex multiple times, and he was as steam-filled as a hot kettle. He was beginning to wonder if it was possible to have his fill of her.

He wasn't through with her yet, and he hoped like hell she wasn't through with him. Once she went home to Florida, he knew that would be it. She'd go back to her life and he would go back to his. She had her sights set on traveling. He was destined for more awards. But he wasn't ready to release her from his hold. Not just yet.

He wished he could read her mind. He sure as hell couldn't read her expression.

"You're not done writing the article," he said, figuring that was true. "Isn't there more you need from me?"

Her smile was slight, but it gave him hope.

"I'll keep bringing you coffee in the morning," he said into her hair. She reinvigorated him, made him feel new. Fresh ideas had been bouncing around in his head since she'd climbed into bed with him. "You're inspiring."

She sat up on an elbow and this time he read her doubtful expression clearly.

"I'm not feeding you a line," he argued with the accusation in her eyes. "Come back here."

She muttered something about him being "impossible" but snuggled into him again, this time lying on her side and draping her arm over his chest.

"I haven't felt this alive in a long time," He rested his chin on the top of her head. The smoke above had cleared, revealing a sea of twinkling stars. "You make me better, Pres. At everything."

But no matter how much she meant to him, he had to have limits with her. How could he possibly ask her to trust him after he'd demolished her trust so thoroughly? After he had proven his success came first, regardless of what she'd meant to him.

"I'm sure Delilah would give me a week's extension to close some of the gaps in my article," she said.

"And you can write about the new song I'm recording next week."

"A new song?" He heard the excitement in her voice. He loved how much she loved his music. It was the highest honor. "Which one?"

"One you haven't heard." He kissed the top of her head. "But you will. I mean, if you stay."

He felt her smile on his bare chest. "You're such a tease."

"Not teasing." If anyone was teasing, she was teasing *him*. She was giving him everything he wanted that he couldn't keep. Everything he shouldn't have left behind and couldn't get back.

Those were sad words, cut him right to the core. But they were also honest. He mentally noted to add them to his new song. No one knew better than him that heartbreak was a big seller.

"If you're sure?" She was back to tracing circles on his chest again—his favorite sensation. Her fingers, his bare chest, her soft exhalations tickling his skin.

Another boat motored by as a shooting star streaked across the sky.

"Yeah, Pres. I'm sure."

Sixteen

"This is your job," Presley said to herself, her eyes on her laptop. "Do your job."

The cursor on the screen waited for her decision. She bit her lip, reread the email for the umpteenth time and doubted herself anew.

"This is what you came here to find out," she whispered. "So, *find out*."

Granted, she hadn't planned on emailing Heather Bell. It just so happened the new intern at Viral Pop came across Heather's private email. Ray was very much Team Presley when it came to the content contest. She appreciated his having her back, and saw no harm in attempting contact with the actress. She was running out of time.

In the email to Heather, Presley played up how

she was helping repair Cash's reputation with his fans. She also might have told a teensy-*weensy* lie about how she and Cash were a couple. She'd even hinted at the idea of "ring shopping" this week, which, admittedly, was a little over the top. But if Heather believed Presley and Cash were serious, that might help sell the assumption that Pres had his best interests at heart. Which she did, ultimately. In her defense, it wasn't an out-and-out lie. She was technically "coupling" with him.

Presley also mentioned assisting with media attention for Heather's upcoming TV series by promising Heather a timely interview. Whether or not the actress trusted or believed Presley, Heather had to be familiar with Viral Pop. The amount of exposure wouldn't be small and could definitely boost any career.

Finger hovering over the send button, Presley tapped Send and sat back, feeling moderately satisfied with her many justifications.

The back door swung open and in walked a dripping-wet Cash, rubbing his hair with a towel. His lashes were spiked, rivulets of water running down his naked chest and over the bumps of his ab muscles. He looked ridiculously hot. He rarely didn't. Lake water rained off his board shorts and soaked the rug by the door.

"Hey," he said.

She slammed her laptop lid down guiltily. "Hey! How was your swim?"

"Wet. You busy?"

"Nope!" She stood and stuffed her hands into her shorts pockets, worried he might read the guilt on her face. "I was about to take a break."

"Good. Water's warm. Come swim with me."

Why was it whenever he commanded she "come" do anything, she did it? Staying in his house, or in his bed the way she had last night, put her directly in the path of an emotional tornado. Not that she could, or would, take cover.

Whenever his dark eyes were trained on hers, she remembered why she came to him. She'd forgotten what it was like to have his undivided attention. It was heady.

When she was within arm's reach, his arm snapped out and tugged her against his wet, warm body. Water soaked through her gauzy white cover-up and then that was gone when he lifted it over her head and tossed it on the floor. Then he was carrying her outside to his sandy, man-made beach at the edge of the water.

"Watch for sharp sticks," he advised, settling her into the waist-deep water.

"I can't think of anything to say that's not dirty." The sun kissed her skin, the water as warm as promised.

"Well, by all means." He scooped her up again and carried her deeper into the water. "Don't hold back on my account."

"Throw me," she instructed, reaching up to hold her nose.

"Yeah?"

She nodded and he adjusted his hold, first giving her a pinch on the butt, before tossing her a few feet into the air. She squeezed her eyes closed, hit the water with a splash and resurfaced with a smile.

He was laughing and coming toward her again. He caught her easily. This time when he lifted her, he kissed her mouth hard.

"Wildcat," he accused.

Yep, she was falling in love with him again.

He didn't toss her but held her against his warm, solid body. She wrapped her legs around his waist and pressed herself flush to his torso.

"Hmm," she said, nuzzling his nose with hers, "I think I found one of those sharp sticks you were talking about."

"Tree trunk, baby. Tree trunk."

She threw her head back and laughed. He was too much. Too hot, too funny, too sexy, too good at absolutely everything. He was her specific brand of catnip. He drove her crazy in the best way possible, and she didn't think he was even trying.

"Mom and Dad are having a family barbecue on Saturday. You're invited."

"I am?"

"Course you are. They want to meet you."

Gulp.

"That's thoughtful." And terrifying. How should she introduce herself? *Hi, I'm Cash's ex-girlfriend who refused to sleep with him only now we're doing it nonstop and it's great. By the way, I'm also sniff-*

ing around to find and expose a secret he's never told anyone.

She couldn't shake the guilt about the damn email. Maybe there wasn't anything to worry about. Her request might go unanswered or be lost in Heather's spam folder for eternity. Once she received a response, she'd know how to approach Cash. Although she might want to write her own version of his apology song, in case he wasn't feeling magnanimous.

"Did you see how Hallie reacted when you brought up Gavin?" she asked, mainly to stop her incessant worrying.

Predictably, Cash's eyebrows lowered in confusion. "How do you mean?"

"She likes him. *Likes* him, likes him."

"You could tell that by talking to her for a few minutes last night?"

"A woman knows."

"Is that so?" He watched her for a long beat that felt almost accusatory thanks to her guilty conscience. "I don't know, Pres. She's the consummate good girl and Gavin…"

"Gavin what?"

"Gavin's not interested in settling down."

"Seems to run in the family. I mean, except for Will. But his 'one' was Hannah Banks, so what choice did he have?"

"She's a force. And, as you've noticed, Hallie isn't like her."

Presley's neck jerked. "Are you saying Hallie

can't handle the likes of *Gavin*? He's charming and friendly and—"

"With you, maybe." Cash frowned, seeming irked at her list of compliments about his youngest brother.

"With me, definitely. He offered to let me stay with him first. He's nice."

Cash's visage darkened, even in the bright sunshine. He adjusted his hold on her, his hands wrapped tight at her thighs. "He was being *nice* so you'd stay in his house with him."

"What? No, he wasn't."

"Gavin is charming and friendly, but he also likes his relationships short and sweet. If Hallie's smart she'll stay away from him."

Well, Presley knew firsthand that "smart" had nothing to do with it.

"No way was Gavin trying to convince me to stay with him. He gave in with hardly a fight when you demanded I stay with you."

"I demanded?"

She ignored that. "And anyway I'm not interested in Gavin the way I'm interested in…"

Cash grinned, satisfied that she'd walked into his trap.

"I'm not interested in Gavin."

"Good." Cash stamped his mouth on hers.

"How could you be jealous of Gavin—" she twirled her fingers in Cash's hair, where a few unruly curls looped at the base of his neck "—when I'm here with you?"

"Presley," he groaned, and she felt her belly drop in delicious anticipation.

"Yes?"

"Honey, get ready."

"Ready for what?"

He untangled her arms from his neck, kissed one of her palms and murmured, *"This."*

Then the bastard tossed her into the air. Before she had a chance to hold her nose, she splashed into the lake water. When she surfaced this time, she was sputtering and he was laughing.

She swam after him, catching him before he could dive beneath the water. She climbed on his back and dunked him, satisfied with her payback. But when he exploded out of the water and pressed her against his front, she wondered if she'd ever truly be satisfied when it came to Cash.

Eventually she'd leave Beaumont Bay and resume a new life of pay raises and wanderlust. She'd probably forget all about him once she was stationed in Italy or France.

But then he kissed her, opening his mouth to allow his warm tongue to tangle with hers, and she knew she'd been lying to herself all morning.

Forgetting him would take more than a trip overseas. She wasn't sure a trip to Mars could erase Cash from her memory bank, but she was still going to try her damnedest to forget about him.

Seventeen

The rest of the week zoomed by.

Presley and Cash had developed a routine of sorts. Coffee on the deck, although sometimes he brought her coffee to bed. His bed, since she hadn't slept in the guest room since the Fourth of July.

Once she was out of bed, they'd either sit side by side and write on the dock, or if it was raining, at the kitchen counter instead. She'd had trouble focusing since Cash was plain distracting. Whether perched on a stool and singing bits and pieces of the song he was composing, or chewing on his pencil while reading his notes, his bare feet resting on the bottom rung of the stool. Just completely distracting.

Yesterday afternoon his low, rocky voice had stolen her attention from her writing. She'd leaned on one elbow and stared at his beautiful profile while he stumbled, started and stumbled again. He'd shot her a grin, but it faded when he noticed her staring.

"What?" he'd asked.

"You're so talented. It would have been a waste for you to have become a football player. Or if you'd pursued the business side of music like your brothers. You'd have robbed everyone of your incredible voice. I've never heard anyone who sounded like you."

"Pres—"

"I mean it." She turned on her stool to face him. "You sing and I forget the world around me. I'm completely lost in your music. Not everyone has that ability. Just you."

He blew out a breath from his nose, his fingers curling around the neck of his guitar. The rain picked up, beating the windowpanes and painting the outside a moody gray-blue.

"Get over here," he'd told her. She'd hopped off her stool at the same time he left his. He set the guitar on a stand in the living room and then pulled her onto the couch with him.

First, she'd been on top, his rough jaw scraping her soft skin while he made out with her long and slow. Then he'd reversed their positions and pressed her into the leather cushions. They'd kissed for a long, long while as distant thunder rumbled. They'd advanced to heavy petting by the time the storm blew in.

She'd climaxed with his mouth on her nipple, his

fingers in her underwear. Then she'd pushed him onto his back, and tried something she hadn't experienced with him yet. She kissed a trail from his chest to his flat stomach and took him into her mouth.

She loved the heft of him, the taste of him on her tongue. She loved more the way she'd driven him to the brink. He nearly lost control but had stopped to haul her up by the elbows and kiss her deep and hard. They'd made love on the couch, but that hadn't been hard or fast. Their lazy pace had matched the ebbing rain outside.

It was a memory of their rainy-day lovemaking that consumed her on Saturday morning. Not the sexy shower or the way they'd slept curled into each other afterward. They'd savored one another.

Like they both knew the end was coming.

When she'd first arrived in Beaumont Bay, she hadn't expected to miss Cash when she left, but now she didn't see how to keep from it. He was…consuming. And the last thing she wanted was to be consumed by anyone.

She climbed out of his comfy bed and carried her empty coffee cup downstairs, humming Cash's new song, "Back for Good."

He'd been piecing it together all week, and had finally laid down a track he and Will were happy with. It was by far her favorite song from the new album. It was soulful and, when sang in his rough, low, damn sexy voice, practically *orgasmic*. Since he'd sung it on repeat this week, and then several times in the studio while she'd watched and listened, the tune was on a loop in her head.

In the kitchen she hummed the chorus, passing by Cash, who stood, his back to her while he looked outside. Capable, attentive, sexy Cash. It really was too bad she was leaving for home tomorrow. Delilah had been generous about giving Pres extra time, but she needed to be back in the office for the release of the article. An article that didn't have much of a chance of winning the coveted pay raise and internship. Not without the scandalous reveal she'd been plotting—she hadn't heard a peep from Heather.

Not that Pres would have revealed the truth anyway.

Last night, while she listened to him sing his heart out, she'd decided to stop trying to figure out the inspiration behind "Lightning." She'd written a robust article about Elite Records, with an exclusive behind-the-scenes peek at Cash recording his new album. She had weaved in details about the way he was at home—leaving out that she'd shared his bed, of course. And she'd outlined how generous he was with fans whenever they bumped into him downtown.

The fresh focus of her article had nothing to do with scandal or secrets, but she was proud of it anyway. It would give readers an honest look at an honest man, and whet their appetites for his next big hit. There was no way "Back for Good" wouldn't go to number one.

If the new angle of her article cost her the contest,

she would simply have to find another way to convince Delilah to grant the raise and transfer Presley deserved. Pres had known deep down she wasn't doing the right thing, and the guilt had been eating her alive. She wasn't going to sneak around behind Cash's back anymore, not after how intimate they'd been. Not after that sexy afternoon on the sofa when their very souls had been involved in the exchange.

She cared about him too much to hurt him. The decision had set her heart at ease.

As she refilled her coffee mug she became aware of a searing gaze on the side of her head. She turned to find Cash watching her, his phone pressed to his ear and his expression fierce. He didn't give her a panty-melting smile nor did he deliver a cheeky wink. And he didn't crook a finger and invite her to come to him.

His shadowed brow matched the low-hanging clouds outside. His frown, edged by a day's worth of growth on his jaw and cheeks, was just as dark. He was *pissed* and that sent a shimmer of fear down her spine.

"Guess who just walked into the room?" he said into the phone. His eyes narrowed to slits fringed by thick, black eyelashes as he watched her round the counter. "You guessed it. My *fiancée,* Presley Cole. You want to say hi?"

He offered the phone but she leaped away from it like he'd offered her a live rattlesnake. Evidently, Heather had read the email and had taken that "ring shopping" hint to heart. Explanations and excuses piled up in Presley's mind.

"Never mind." He returned the phone to his ear. "She can't talk right now."

True. Her mouth might as well be stuffed with cotton balls for how speechless she felt.

He said goodbye, lowered the phone and prowled over to her. She backed up a step for every one he advanced. Until she bumped into the countertop and she uttered a weak, "Ow."

She expected him to yell at her, which she deserved, but maybe she could explain herself before he started. Explain how she was no longer planning on writing about "Lightning" at all. How she had already written the piece and had instead focused on his new album. How she was telling the story of how amazing he was with his fans and his brothers—

"Heather Bell and I had a physical relationship and nothing more," he boomed, speaking first and robbing her of the chance. "Unlike Carla, who gave me the physical but could also hold a conversation."

Presley's stomach did a barrel roll.

"Heather was so far in my rearview I didn't expect to hear from her again. *Ever.* We burned hot, but fast. And then it was over." His eyebrows were two angry slashes as he went on. "Imagine my surprise when she calls to tell me a reporter is asking if Heather inspired my song 'Lightning.' Excuse me, not a reporter. My *fiancée!*" He roared the word and Presley winced.

"Cash, listen to me. I didn't think she'd focus on

what you and I were to each other. I just hoped she'd trust me enough to—"

"You could have asked *me*," he growled.

She flinched. Not because he was scaring her, but because he was right. She could have. She *should* have.

"You and me in my bed, on my boat, on my couch while it rained, Presley."

His words, and the hurt lingering in the depth of his eyes were as good as an accusation. He'd trusted her, and now it appeared as if she'd slept with him solely to gain his trust. Why hadn't she just been honest in that damn email?

Because you never dreamed Heather would call him and rat you out. A huge oversight, to be sure.

Her heart sank as tears warmed the backs of her eyes. Heather's timing couldn't have been worse. Pres had wanted to find the truth, but sleeping with him had never been about playing him. Now how was she supposed to convince him otherwise?

"So this—" he tossed his cell phone onto the counter "—is what you're doing when you're not having sex with me?"

"Cash, I swear," she started but he cut her off again.

"You reached out to my ex-girlfriend and asked her instead of coming to me." His voice, quiet but lethal, was ten times scarier than when he'd been shouting.

He loomed over her, fists balled at his sides. Guilt

made her defenses climb sky-high. Rather than sing her version of his apology song, she yelled back at him.

"Would you have told me if I'd asked you?"

He straightened his spine and said nothing.

"That's what I thought." She folded her arms. "What do you care if the world knows if you sang 'Lightning' about Heather, or Carla, or both of them? It's just gossip anyway. No matter what some reporter writes or doesn't write, you could deny it."

"Don't you mean whatever *my fiancée* writes?"

"I was trying to sound credible. That was wrong," she admitted, her voice small.

"You think? The meaning behind that song is personal, Presley, and none of the world's goddamn business. I'm not protecting myself. I'm protecting the woman I wrote the song about. I've performed it a thousand times and I'm the only one who knows. I *like* that I'm the only one who knows."

He wasn't yelling anymore, but watching her with sad eyes. And instantly she knew she'd made a big mistake.

"You're protecting her?"

He didn't respond. He didn't have to. His disappointed expression said it all.

"From people like me," she concluded. "Ugh."

She sank on one of the stools at the counter, her head hanging. Even though she'd changed her mind about pursuing the truth, at one point she'd intended to write that story. Somehow, she'd become the kind of person she least respected. A reporter who would compromise everything to get the story. Including her own integrity. The truth, in Cash's case, wasn't hers to share.

Double ugh.

"For what it's worth, I gave up trying to find out."

He was silent, but still looming. She peeked up at him.

"You put people ahead of yourself a lot," she pointed out. His hands rested on the countertop and she admired his knuckles. His blunt nails. The hair on his forearms. How was it that every inch of him was undeniably attractive? She thought of his hands and his arms on another woman. Knowing he'd written "Lightning" about someone he'd cared about deeply made her want to wail. But this wasn't about her.

"Honestly, Pres. What were you thinking?"

"I wasn't." She let out a defeated breath. "I'm sorry. I was just…carried away. Blind ambition and all that," she said, which sounded like an excuse even to her own ears. "That probably sounds lame."

He let out a deep sigh. "Believe it or not, I understand how chasing success can make you do something stupid."

Was he talking about the way he'd left her in Florida to chase his own success? That seemed like too much of a leap, so she instead rerouted to ask, "Do you want me to stay home today rather than go with you to the barbecue?"

She'd been looking forward to spending the day with the Sutherland family, and not only because she'd planned on snapping a few candid photos for her article while she was there. She wanted to meet Cash's parents, hang out with Hannah, who was arriving with Will. And she'd wanted to say goodbye to Luke and Gavin, and Hallie if she showed up. But, given her egregious behavior, she wouldn't blame Cash if he disinvited her.

His hand cupped the nape of her neck and he looked down on her, sadness still swimming in his eyes. Then he bent and kissed the crown of her head.

"We leave at noon." He let her go and walked to the staircase.

"Cash?"

He paused at the foot of the stairs, head down, fists clenched.

"Are you all right?"

He didn't look at her. He simply repeated, "Noon."

Eighteen

In his parents' backyard, Cash sat, a glass of iced tea sweating in his hand. His brothers surrounded him in a semicircle. Dad manned the grill, chatting with their mom, Dana, who micromanaged Dad in her own irritating, sweet way. Travis Sutherland informed his wife of this moments before he dipped her over one arm and kissed her. Dana giggled and swatted him when he set her on her feet again.

Cash didn't feel like smiling, but he smiled. His parents had such a laidback, loving relationship. How did they do it?

Though he'd been trying to shake it, frustration coated him like a sheen of oil. As pissed off as he was that Presley had circumvented him and lied, he knew there was nothing evil behind her intentions. Oversights happened. He knew how badly she wanted to win. At one point he'd been as blindly ambitious as she was, and it'd cost him the ultimate price: *her*. How could he fault her for doing the same now without being a total hypocrite?

He wanted to believe she'd have come to him before running the article. He was angrier that she'd been poking around about "Lightning" at all. The truth—that Presley had inspired the song he'd written while high on heartbreak after their brief relationship—was one he'd intended to take to his grave.

He'd been in love with her back then. In love and in complete denial. Until they'd made love on his couch, the rain hitting the windows behind him, did he realize what he'd lost to her. That hollow, empty feeling in his chest was because his missing heart had gone to Presley Cole.

He'd been so focused on his dreams back when they'd been in college, on escaping the football-and-business degree trajectory he'd been on, that he'd been single-minded about leaving. He'd convinced himself then that what he and Pres had shared was too short-lived to be real and lasting love. Only in hindsight had he realized he'd blown it with her, and only recently had he realized that falling in love with her was easy when he'd never fallen out.

"Things are going good," Luke, his hand wrapped around a beer bottle resting on his knee, remarked.

Cash jerked out of his thoughts and focused on his brother. "At the bar?"

"No, man. With your girl. Things are going good with Presley."

Cash followed his brother's gaze across the yard to where Presley stood with Hannah and Hallie. Pres was wearing a green dress with tiny pink flowers on it, and a pair of bright white sneakers. Her hair was back in a ponytail, showing off her cute ears and sun-kissed cheekbones. She was girl-next-door irresistible, but capable of being his bad girl whenever he slipped her out of her clothes. And when she made mistakes, she apologized for them. She tried to make everything right even when it didn't serve her best interests.

She was perfect.

"She's going home tomorrow," Cash told Luke. No matter how perfect she was, or how he felt about her, she wasn't staying.

"And you're letting her?" Luke chuffed.

"This proves it," Gavin butted in. "I'm the smart one. You let her go again, you're an idiot."

Cash sipped his iced tea and decided silence was his best ally. At this rate his *only* ally. Then he opened his mouth to defend himself anyway. "She was never staying. You knew that."

"I didn't know you'd talk her into staying longer and show up in town with her hand in yours." Gavin's eyebrows lifted, daring Cash to argue.

"Florida's not that far away," Luke commented. "It's a day's drive. A shorter flight."

"And when would I have time to drive or fly to

Florida?" Irritated, Cash shifted in his lawn chair. "Between albums? Or during the tour?"

"Damn, sorry I brought it up." Luke took a swig from his beer.

So was Cash. His darkest worry was that a precious part of Presley would forever hate him for leaving her that dark night in her dorm room. That she'd never truly trust him since she knew firsthand he was capable of walking away and never looking back.

"Meat's done, thank God. I'm starving," Will announced, rejoining his brothers. "Damn. What did I miss? Cash looks grumpier than usual. What are you worried about? We have the album on lock. You guys hear 'Back for Good' yet?" he asked Gav and Luke.

"Yeah," Luke confirmed at the same time Gavin said, "Not yet."

"Well, you should. I think Presley's right," Will said. "She thinks it should be Cash's first single."

"It's a ballad," Luke said, wrinkling his nose. "Guess it depends on the month it drops."

"Country music is nothing but ballads and bar songs," Gavin put in.

"It's a hit. Trust me," Will said.

Sick of everyone talking about him like he wasn't sitting there, Cash barked, "I'm trashing that song."

"What?" Will asked, predictably incensed.

"You heard me. I'm rewriting it. That track we laid down is no good."

"No good? Are you insane?"

"Yes," Gavin and Luke answered in tandem.

"I can't let you do that, man," Will stated.

"It's happening," Cash informed him. "I'm rewriting 'Back for Good.' It's a shit song and I can do better."

A lie. "Back for Good" was one of his best. But it was too honest. And it depressed the hell out of him considering it would never come to pass.

"Are you insane?" came a sharp, feminine voice from behind.

This time Will, Gavin and Luke all said "Yes" at the same time.

Cash turned to find Presley coming from the direction of the house, a dish of potato salad in her hands. Behind her, Hannah and Hallie completed their journey to the picnic table.

"I can't let you rewrite that song," Presley said.

"That's what I said," Will agreed.

Presley only had eyes for Cash. "That's the best song on the album so far. Hell, it might be your best song *ever*. Even better than 'Lightning.'"

"That's a big statement," Gavin said.

"You must not have heard it yet," she challenged before her gaze jerked back to Cash.

"Ladies and gentlemen, start moving to the picnic table. Time to eat!" Travis hollered.

"Give us a sec." Cash slid a meaningful glare to his brothers.

Luke stood, Gavin with him. Will snagged the bowl from Presley's hands and followed his brothers, granting Cash and Presley a dab of privacy while the family arranged themselves on the long wooden benches.

"It was a mistake to contact Heather," Presley said. "I didn't expect her to call you. I really am sorry."

"It's done, Pres."

"'Back for Good' is the best song I've ever heard and I'm not just saying that. Your fans deserve to hear it."

He wedged his teeth together.

"Back for Good" was a fantasy. And he'd been a fool to believe he'd release that song and proceed to sing it for years to come without thinking of and missing the redhead gazing up at him now. "Back for Good," like "Lightning," was inspired by Presley. Except "Back for Good" was the happy ending to the sad story "Lightning" had started.

How the hell was he supposed to tell her *that*? Especially when their story ended with her leaving him this time around.

"We're about to say grace, Cash," Travis called.

"Coming," Cash stood. "Pres, let it go."

She didn't.

"I forbid you from changing a single note of that song. A single *word*." She touched the center of his chest.

He leaned in close, his nose almost touching hers. "That's not up to you."

"I'm your muse so it kind of is." She poked him as she spoke as if punctuating each word.

"Seriously guys, I'm starving," Luke offered. "You know Dad won't let us eat until we pray."

Cash ignored him.

Presley's features softened. "I'm going home tomorrow and I'm going to publish an article about Cash Sutherland, the man. A man who is dedicated to his craft, his family and his friends. I'm going to share your writing process and what it was like to be there when inspiration struck you in the middle of dinner. Or while you're making coffee in the morning." She blushed when she added, "And other times, but I won't share those. Not with anyone.

"I'm going to show your fans you're more than a sex symbol or an award-winning performer." Her hand flattened on his chest. "I'm going to show them you. The real you. And when they see that, they're going to forget about the mug shot and the bogus DUI. And if they don't forget, they won't care. Not once they see the guy beneath the glitz."

His heart sank. The longer she talked, the more sincere she sounded, and the worse she made everything. She had no idea how hard she was making it for him to let her go when all he wanted to do was beg her to stay. How could he ask her to trust him again after how badly he'd abused that trust? Simple. He couldn't.

"Don't forget the part about how I walk on water," he muttered.

Her gentle touch, her profession that she loved his song and forbade he change a word of it, was too much to take. Especially when a profession dwelled deep inside him—an "I love you" he wouldn't dare speak.

No matter how sweet her words were, or how true the sentiment behind them, he knew she wouldn't take a chance on him again. The hell of it was, he couldn't blame her. A few weeks of bliss wasn't enough to erase years of hurt. She'd built her own life, separate from his, and she deserved to live it. Even if he could coax her into coming back for good like he sang in his new song, he wouldn't make her choose between him and her dreams. Hadn't he been selfish enough for a lifetime?

"Do you hear me?" She had to know he'd heard every word she'd said since he hadn't taken his eyes off her yet. "I'm not writing about 'Lightning' and if you like, I'll call Heather Bell and personally apologize. I'm not going to *out* whoever you wrote that song about, Cash. I…care about you. I have always cared about you."

And he cared about her—still. He'd laid himself bare in "Back for Good." He'd written snippets of it when Presley was in his bed, in his arms. When she'd been sunbathing on his deck. He'd been consumed and inspired and, what was the word? Oh, right. *Stupid.* He'd been stupid to pretend for a second he could allow this fairy tale to go on.

"Cash, honey," this from his mother. "I'm sorry to interrupt."

His mom wasn't the least bit sorry, but evidently he wasn't going to have the chance to finish this damn conversation without interruption.

"We're coming," Presley called cheerily, snatching his hand and dragging him to the table.

"Finally!" Gavin said, reaching for the potato salad.

"Not yet," Travis scolded. "Grace."

While his father said grace, Cash bowed his head, but he wasn't paying attention to the prayer. He'd been arriving at a decision. Tonight, once he returned to his house with Presley, he'd tell her the truth.

It was time for the fantasy to end. She wanted to know the inspiration behind "Lightning"? He'd tell her. She could share it with the world and claim the prize at work. It was the least he owed her for leaving her in the dust years ago. And, if he were being honest with himself, it wasn't only his secret. It was hers to do with what she wanted.

He'd leave out the part where he still regretted leaving her. He wouldn't admit he knew he'd ruined his one shot. And he sure as shit wasn't going to tell her that "Back for Good" was inspired by what could have been. It was a great song, but he'd see to it that it never saw the light of day.

He'd do that for her. Because of what he'd seen shimmering in her eyes as she'd begged him not to change a word of that song.

Love.

He saw it now, and he'd seen it on the couch yesterday. While they'd spent long, intimate moments together as it rained cats and dogs. He'd felt it, too, eating into him. It was heavy and undeniable, but he had to deny it.

He'd had his shot. His flash. Like his own song said, lightning never struck the same place twice. He didn't deserve her forgiveness for the mistake he made years ago. Arguably he hadn't deserved her company while she was here.

Whatever chance they might've had was over. He refused to hurt her twice.

Nineteen

On the drive home from his family's house, Presley chatted about his brothers and how good his parents' cooking tasted. Cash seemed a million miles away, giving one-word answers rather than committing to conversation.

She didn't want to leave town on a low note, but she was leaving in less than twelve hours, so that was a definite possibility. She was fairly certain he was still upset with her for contacting Heather, and honestly, Presley understood why. What she'd done hadn't been nefarious or calculated, but it'd been a breach of trust.

Hopefully by the time she left he would be able to forgive her for it.

At his house, he parked in the garage and rounded

the sleek sports car to open her door for her. She followed him into the kitchen, intending to revisit the conversation they'd started at his family's house. She couldn't let him even *consider* rewriting "Back for Good." She *forbade* it. It was his best work and she should know. She was a Cash Sutherland superfan from way back. From before he was *The* Cash Sutherland.

Rather than put off this discussion another second, she faced him and asked, "Do you believe me?"

He tossed the car keys on the counter and then ran a hand through his hair. "About what?"

"About me not writing about who inspired 'Lightning.' I mean, I still don't know who inspired it, but if I did, the secret would be safe with me. I promise not to mention Carla or Heather."

He watched her for so long, she wasn't sure if he'd fallen asleep with his eyes open, or zoned out while thinking of something else. Either of those possibilities would have been more expected than what came next.

He closed the gap between them, leveled his eyes with hers by bending slightly and hugged her neck with one palm. "I wrote 'Lightning' after I left FSU. I wrote it about the shot I could have had if I hadn't left behind the woman I loved. I wrote it, Presley Cole, about *you*."

Lost in his dark, penetrating gaze, especially since he hadn't moved so much as an inch away from her, she had to blink to break the spell. His expression bordered on agonized and she felt similar. She had no witty response in her toolkit to deal with his admission.

"M-me?"

"We had something then, but I was too young and stupid to see it. I had big dreams and goals and I couldn't handle being in love and pursuing those dreams. I was too tangled up in my own circumstances. In one fell swoop I erased the possibility of a football career, dropped out of college and left Florida for Tennessee. Left you. In short, Pres, I fucked up. And that's what 'Lightning' is about. We had a shot. I blew it."

With a sigh, he stopped touching her and walked away. She watched him unlock one of the French doors and step outside. Numbly, she struggled to wrap her feeble mind around what he'd told her. He…loved her back then?

She'd listened to "Lightning" on the radio every time she'd come across it, and that song got a ton of airplay. She knew every word. She'd cranked it and sang along loudly, often with the top off her Jeep. She'd bobbed her head to the music while she sat at her desk with her headphones on. She'd *ached* over those lyrics, remembering how she'd felt about him back then and lamenting that she hadn't touched him as deeply. More than once she'd wished "Lightning" was about her. Wished that Cash had felt an iota of what he felt for the mystery woman in the song.

And now he was saying *she* was the mystery woman who'd inspired it?

He'd written a love song about lightning striking

once, yet here she stood. In his house, hours away from leaving for Florida, and completely, irrevocably in love with him yet again.

And apparently, he was content to let her leave.

She yanked the door open and marched out to the dock, where Cash stood, silently staring out at the lake. Clouds hung low in the sky, and without the help of stars and the moon, the water appeared murky black.

"Weather's clearing up tomorrow," he said without turning around. "You should have decent roads for traveling out of the mountains. Are you going straight through or will you stop for an overnight on the way down?"

Instead of responding to his irritatingly detached words, she stated, "You weren't in love with me in college."

He faced her, his arms crossed, his expression neutral. So, she went on.

"When you broke up with me, you told me you were leaving everything behind in Florida, including me. You told me I'd be okay because we'd never been serious. You told me you had fun with me and that you hoped I didn't regret the time I spent with you."

Time they'd spent being intimate but never going past the point of no return. Time they'd spent together *not* having sex, which she sometimes believed was the reason he'd been able to walk away without looking back.

"You had no regrets, Cash." Her voice shook. She almost needed that to be true. The alternative was unbelievable. "I spent the entire next year wishing I would have slept with you, wondering if you would have stayed with me then. And now you're telling me your most popular love song is about me?"

"I had regrets, Presley. You didn't corner the market on those." His stubborn jaw was set. "I wrote about them in that song."

She replayed the lyrics in her head. The part about his walking away when he knew lightning struck only once. About not being able to catch lightning in a bottle so he'd had to let it go. The part about how he'd never have again what he'd found all those years ago.

"I was in love with you back then," she said, not willing to admit she was now, too.

"I know." She could read the regret in his features. It glowed like the neon in a sign.

"And you're saying…you loved me, too? But you didn't stick around. You didn't tell me. You let me believe I was this…this…silly, naïve girl who fell in love with a guy who didn't give a damn about me!"

"I thought a clean break would be easier for both of us," he countered, his voice raised. "I had a lot to deal with back then, Pres."

"Oh, did you? You had a lot to deal with coming home to your beautiful family and living in the lap of luxury while you found yourself? Meanwhile, I was heartbroken and trying to pick up the pieces of a life I didn't recognize anymore, while trying not to fail every exam that next quarter. And then I slept with someone hoping I'd finally get over you and you're telling me the whole time that you were in love with me and *you left anyway*?"

Sick. She was going to be sick. She'd wasted not only the time they'd dated, but years after thinking of him. For a while she'd pined for him, for a longer while she'd mourned. And then when she was finally over him, she'd traveled to Beaumont Bay and allowed herself to be talked into his bed.

You're smarter than this, Presley.

"What was your plan this time around, Cash? Were you testing a theory? Or did you need inspiration for another hit song? Don't tell me you were actually hoping I'd be 'Back for Good'?"

His head snapped up and his mouth pulled into a frown.

"My God." She wasn't as far off the mark as she'd hoped. "Is that what your new song is about? Me staying?"

"Presley."

"But I'm leaving. An-and you're encouraging me to go. Is this a game to you? Do you enjoy stringing me along and then pushing me away?"

"Pres, listen to me."

Which begged another question. "Why did you tell me about 'Lightning'?"

He licked his lips. Sucked in a deep breath. "You gave up New York."

She blinked. "What?"

"The internship. You stayed in Florida because I was in Florida. Your grades were slipping. Because of me."

She shook her head, but the sentiment was weak. She wanted to accuse him of being cocky and self-centered, but she *had* turned down New York for him. She had put her life on hold once she was in his orbit. That's what you did when you loved someone. Or at least, that's what *she* did.

"I can't give you anything else, but I can give you the truth. Now you know the answer to the question behind who inspired 'Lightning.' Do with it what you will. If it helps your career and allows you to travel the world like you dreamed, then maybe I can live with myself for letting you leave. If it's a secret you want to keep to yourself, so be it. I'm not telling anyone."

"You can't give me anything else," she repeated, her voice trembling with anger. "What the hell does that mean?" But she knew. He'd clearly said he was letting her leave—that he could live with himself now that he'd told her the truth. But what about her? What about what the truth was going to do to *her*? He'd practically guaranteed she would spend years pining and yearning and mourning him all over again.

"I know it was a mistake to let you go, Pres. I do. I know you care about me. I also know that you never truly forgave me for walking away from you. And I don't blame you. Not one damn bit. I was so focused on my own success, I left and didn't look back. You'd be crazy to trust me again."

She was stunned silent, her heart aching at the truth behind those words. The truth was she had struggled to forgive him. And even though she told herself she had, it was hard to trust him now.

"You've heard 'Lightning,' you know how I feel about you."

"Felt," she corrected. "That song was about our past, not the present. And I'm not sure what to think of 'Back for Good.' Was it some warped fantasy or did those feelings from years ago come up again recently?"

Her heart hammered as she waited for him to answer. Those feelings had definitely resurfaced for her. And now, hours before she was heading home, he decided to drop a bomb on her, and for what? His own egotistical reasoning? So he could pay his penance for leaving her back then by telling her the most inconvenient truth ever?

"Songs are one of two things for me," he said. "Fantasy or remembering. 'Lightning' is me remembering who we were, what we had before our lives happened to us. 'Back for Good' is the fairy-tale ending to 'Lightning.'"

"What's so unbelievable about me coming back for good?" She had to ask, at least once.

"This isn't real." He shook his head. "That's why I'm rewriting the song." He delivered her the felling blow on a butterfly's wing. "I was caught up in the fairy tale of you in my bed and back in my life."

"You were caught up," she repeated, her limbs going numb. A protective instinct. She didn't want to feel this pain—couldn't handle it. "And telling me the truth behind 'Lightning' is what, my parting gift?"

"Now you know calling my ex-girlfriends won't clear it up for you."

"No, Cash, *you* cleared everything up for me." Tears burned her eyes but she refused to let them fall. "You took the inspiration you needed and now you're through with me. I was just the idiot falling in love with you again."

She stomped inside and jogged to her room, locking the door when she heard his boots on the stairs. He knocked. She ignored him.

He'd already said enough. Too much.

She could have gone home not knowing he'd loved her once and wasted years of their lives—and her virginity in the process. She could have gone a lifetime without knowing that.

But now she knew the truth. Lucky her! She could share his secret and boost her career. Which she was angry enough to do, but she loved him too much to do that to him. He thought he owed her?

He owed her, all right. He owed her his heart.

But nowhere in his speech had he mentioned his feelings for her in the present. It'd been about his healing as he walked away one more time. Cash was cutting her loose so she could move on with her life. Like she didn't know her own heart and mind. Like she needed him to tell her how to proceed.

God, she really was an idiot.

He stopped knocking, giving up after a few minutes. She pulled her suitcase from the closet and threw it on the bed. Once he fell asleep, she'd leave. She'd drive as far as she could without falling asleep at the wheel and then rent a room in whatever hotel was closest.

She wasn't spending another minute in this house with Cash—the man who'd loved her, but not enough to stick around. The man who claimed he wanted her "back for good," but only as fodder for a hit single. As if their sleeping together for the last two weeks had meant nothing.

She should have known better.

She *did* know better.

Apparently, that was a lesson she'd needed to be taught more than once.

Twenty

Cash's beat-up spiral notebook sat next to his right thigh, its pages blowing in the breeze. He watched them flutter, the many lines and scribbles from where he'd been attempting to rewrite "Back for Good" mocking him. A lot of it hadn't worked.

Any of it, in fact.

Presley had left eleven days ago and he'd been a miserable asshole since. Worse, she hadn't said goodbye when she'd left. She'd packed her bags and sneaked out in the early hours of the morning before he'd woken up, or maybe shortly after he'd fallen asleep. He'd called when he noticed her Jeep missing to make sure she was all right, but she hadn't answered.

He'd called over and over again for the last week-plus, but she hadn't answered his calls then, either. On day three of her being away, he'd asked Gavin to check on her for safety's sake. She'd answered Gavin's text to let him know she was home. She'd also made it clear she didn't want to talk to Cash.

He didn't know if she meant she didn't want to talk to him now, or if she meant she didn't want to talk to him ever, but it felt like the latter.

He plucked a few strings and tried out the revised lyrics to "Back for Good." Unsurprisingly, they didn't flow. He set aside his guitar, snatched up his notebook and flung it into the air. It sailed on the breeze before hitting the water, pages open, where it bobbed on the undulating surface.

"I give your form a six, but the distance a solid nine-point-zero." Gavin walked down the dock, hands in his shorts pockets. "Thought I'd find you out here. Writing not going well?"

"You could say that." The notebook sank below the surface, now nothing but bleeding ink and soggy paper held together by a piss-poor spiral coil. Words had meant something to him before Presley left. Now they were meaningless.

His fault. He'd been the one who hadn't given her a reason to stay. Cash walked back to the deck. Gavin followed, Cash's guitar in hand.

"Soft drink sponsorship is a go, by the way." Gavin sat, guitar in his lap, and played a few clumsy chords. "How do you do it, man?"

"Do what?"

"Lay out your feelings so cleanly. Express them

so genuinely in your music. Perform them so openly in front of thousands of strangers." Gavin attempted another few chords before giving up and setting the guitar aside. "You have a gift."

"Keep practicing and you'll get better."

"I'm not only talking about your musical talent, brother. I'm talking about you knowing what's going on in here." Gavin tapped his temple and then his chest. "And in here."

Cash grunted. He didn't know about that.

"What is going on in there when it comes to Presley?" Gavin didn't wait for an answer. "Far as I can see, ever since she left you've been one miserable bastard. And if that's any indication—" he nodded to the spot where Cash had winged the notebook "—you're not having much luck rewriting her song."

"It's not *her* song," Cash lied.

"Yeah, okay. You didn't write 'Back for Good' for the girl you wished was back for good. I heard it. It's your best work."

"I told Will to destroy that track."

"You signed a contract with Elite Records," his music attorney brother reminded him. "Will didn't destroy that track. And you shouldn't force our hand. We'll sue you."

Cash rolled his eyes.

"Nah, we won't," Gav smiled. "But if you change it, I'll be tempted. I can't play or write, but I know a winner when I hear it."

"I don't need to make bank on another Presley Cole–inspired song," he muttered.

"He admits it."

He wasn't admitting anything. Okay, maybe one thing. "I've done a lot I regret. I'm not adding Presley staying when I don't know how it's gonna end to that very long list."

"That crap about artists writing their best stuff when they're depressed is just that. *Crap.* You wrote 'Back for Good' when Presley was here and falling in love with you. And you're pretending like you didn't love her? That's just stupid."

"What it is, is pointless. She's gone, Gav. Look around. She told you she didn't want to speak to me."

His brother said nothing, which in a way was worse. Then he stood, seeming to come up with an idea.

"In that case, you have to start dealing with the heartbreak. And I know one very good way to do that. It might be the only way."

Cash cocked his head. "And that is…"

"Day drinking." Gavin grinned. "I'll drive, so no danger of a DUI."

"You're a funny guy."

"Thanks." Gavin grinned, ignoring Cash's sarcasm.

"Anyway, I'm busy."

"Doing what? Going to throw the guitar in next?" His brother hefted the instrument. "I'd pay to see that."

Cash snatched his guitar. He'd sooner die than sacrifice her to the lake's bottom.

"Luke's at the Cheshire. Asked me to call you

and invite your sorry ass. We'll have the rooftop to ourselves. You could use a break. Bring the guitar. And your notebook. Eh, a new notebook. Maybe inspiration will hit after a few whiskeys."

Cash studied the blue lake and bluer sky, the trees on the horizon. Laughter of vacationers on a boat in the distance carried on the wind. If he wasn't inspired here, he didn't hold out hope for being inspired elsewhere, whiskey or no.

"What's Luke *really* want?" Cash asked, suspicious.

"I'm not supposed to say."

"Gavin."

"He wants you to play the original 'Back for Good' at the Cheshire. I'm supposed to fetch you, bring you there, get you drunk and make sure you agree."

Cash was already shaking his head.

"Don't change the song, Cash. But not because of Will, or Luke, or me. Keep it for the album. For the fans. They deserve the truth. They appreciate that sort of thing, which is why they appreciate you. You're talented, but your superpower is your honesty."

"What about Presley? What does she deserve?"

"She deserves the truth, too."

The truth.

He hadn't been able to admit the truth about her to anyone—not even himself. Maybe that would be the start of healing. Maybe not. Only one way to know for sure. He took a breath before committing, and then said, "Me loving Pres isn't going to change anything. We can't be together for a lot of reasons, the least of them me not telling her how I feel."

"Maybe you're right," Gavin agreed, and Cash realized he'd been hoping his younger brother would argue. He'd hoped for a few reasons to pursue Presley. To try calling her again. To fly down to Florida and beg her to give him a second chance. No. A *third* chance.

Gavin's smile was tight and Cash understood why his brother hadn't encouraged him. Presley must have said more than Gav was letting on.

It was official. Cash had lost her. For good this time.

"Let's go to the Cheshire."

What did he have to lose? His song ideas were at the bottom of Mountain View Lake. Presley wasn't speaking to him. The song he desperately needed to rewrite wasn't coming to him.

If there was ever a time to bury his sorrows in the bottle, it was now.

Delilah rarely smiled the way she'd smiled when Presley's article had been published. Since the timing had coincided with Cash Sutherland and Hannah Banks's duet going gold, the interest in both artists had an organic spike. Presley's article was currently Viral Pop's most popular piece of content.

It'd been picked up and shared countless times on social media. The contest was in the bag, her raise forthcoming and she'd been given the green light to book a flight to wherever in the world she'd like to transfer with the company.

She'd done it.

And it felt nothing like she'd imagined it would. There was no parade, though her fellow writers had surprised her with cupcakes. She'd thanked them, of course, and pasted on a smile, but it was hard to feel celebratory when she'd spent most of her days split between being miserable and angry.

She felt similar to when Cash left the first time, except then she hadn't known what it was like to have sex with him, or be held in his arms all night. Now she did, which made the memories harder to deal with. Especially since she had lost him forever this time.

At least that's what she'd told herself at first.

A few days before the article went live, she'd been rereading it for the umpteenth time, hurting so much she was tempted to take Cash out of the article altogether and focus only on Elite Records and the other Sutherland brothers.

But that would do a disservice to his fans, who deserved to know the man behind the music. So, Presley put her own hurt feelings in the rearview, and poured her heart into the article.

She knew he believed what he'd said about not deserving her forgiveness, but the truth was she was tired of holding onto that grudge—of bearing the oppressive weight of it.

He'd made a mistake. So had she, for similar reasons and far more recently. He'd forgiven her without a second thought. And she hadn't been able to blame her recent bout of selfishness on being a clueless college kid.

But she wasn't the same hearts-in-her-eyes girl she used to be. She'd taken a chance, and had chased her dreams and her heart. Why should she have to choose between them? He'd told her the truth recently, and damn the consequences. She would do the same.

So she wrote the truth about Cash Sutherland. She revealed him for the loving, giving man he was. People didn't need to know who had inspired "Lightning" to understand the sacrifices he'd made for those he loved.

He'd been punishing himself, but also protecting Presley by sending her home to Florida. So focused on doing the right thing for her, he hadn't noticed she didn't need his protection. What she needed, what she deserved, was his heart.

Her article would give him a chance to change his mind.

If he didn't realize what he'd lost this time, then she would book a flight to Viral Pop's London office and she wouldn't look back. She'd traverse the globe. Visit Tokyo. Live in San Francisco for a while. The moon, if the company managed to wrangle an office at Elon Musk's space station. She'd go unhappily, but she'd go knowing she'd left nothing on the table. She'd go knowing she'd said everything. Even if Cash had been the one to sing it first.

Inside the Beaumont Hotel, she pulled off her sunglasses and stepped into the fancy bathroom.

"Déjà vu all over again," she told her reflection in the sitting room. Then she pulled out the bag she'd brought with her so she could freshen up after her long drive from Tallahassee to Tennessee.

Her phone buzzed in her hand and she looked down to see a text from Gavin. There was one word on the screen: Here.

She said a little prayer and then shut herself into a stall to change. She was going to ride the elevator straight up to the Cheshire bar and give Cash one final chance not to blow it.

Then, for better or worse, she'd have her answer.

"What'll it be?" Luke asked as Cash sat on a barstool.

"What are you doing back there?" Cash asked as Gavin sat next to him.

"I like to play bartender on occasion. Revisit my roots. Whiskey?"

"Make his a double," Gavin said.

Luke smiled and poured three doubles, one for each of them.

Hand wrapped around his glass, Cash stared down at his drink for a long moment before Luke pointed out, "You look like something the cat ate, barfed up, ate again and then barfed up again."

Gavin chuckled.

"How go the rewrites?" Luke asked Cash.

"You have any snorkeling gear?" Gavin asked Luke.

Cash grumbled a string of creative swear words

as Gavin explained why snorkeling gear was needed. Luke laughed.

Everyone seemed damned amused by Cash being a sorry sack. He swallowed a mouthful of whiskey. Day drinking was definitely a better idea than writing.

"Will's not going to let you rewrite that song," Luke said. "He'd sooner die."

"That can be arranged." Cash downed the rest of his drink like a shot. Luke did the same and refilled their glasses.

Gavin chugged his and shoved his glass across the bar.

"I know why I'm here," Cash informed Luke.

"Are you serious?" Luke glared at Gavin.

"He knew something was up," Gavin defended.

Luke's eyes narrowed, and next he focused that glare on Cash. "So, he doesn't know everything?"

"Of course not." Gavin sipped from his refilled glass.

Cash looked from Gav to Luke. "What are you—"

"You didn't read it, did you?" Luke pulled his cell phone out of his back pocket and fired off a text. "That'd have been the first thing I'd have done, but I don't have your sense of self-preservation."

Cash's phone dinged and he checked his messages. Luke had sent a link to Viral Pop's website.

"Click it," Gavin advised.

"I know what it says."

"You don't," Luke assured him.

The whiskey must have done its job since Cash

felt curious instead of defiant. He clicked the link. The article opened with a photo of him on his own deck, guitar on his lap. The sun was shining, his now-trashed notebook sitting intact at his side.

Presley had taken that photo. He remembered her asking if she could use it in her article. He'd agreed to let her.

The headline read "Cashing In."

Beneath that read "Everything you wanted to know about singer-songwriter Cash Sutherland. Except for one secret that will forever stay buried."

His heart thudded as he skimmed the article. She didn't write about "Lightning"?

Dammit, he'd gift-wrapped that for her. Then again, if she hated him, she probably didn't want to be hounded by the press about being his inspiration, he thought miserably.

The article began with details about Elite Records and the harrowing rebuild after last season's storms. Then it mentioned Hannah and Cash's duet and how it was sure to bolster the label. She wrote about his struggle following a "bogus" DUI. She cited a source in the Beaumont Bay police department who corroborated that they were investigating the charges, as they'd suspected a faulty Breathalyzer.

By the time he read the words "Back for Good," he saw that Presley had thrown him under the bus as well, stating the song was "the first single from his highly anticipated second album." She then mentioned she'd been granted an early listen, which made him remember her in his bed as he lazily strummed his guitar.

He didn't know how much more he could take, but his brothers clearly weren't going to let up.

"This part." Gavin stabbed the phone's screen. Cash kept reading.

I uncovered the inspiration behind Cash's most famous song. I had my own theories about whom he'd written it about, but his answer surprised me. I have no doubt that if I disclosed the mystery woman, you would be equally surprised. I never saw it coming. And while I could disclose what I've learned, I wouldn't feel right about doing that here. But I do know one thing for sure. Cash's muse loves him to this day, and she'd light her whole world on fire to be his forever. No regrets.

There was more to the article but Cash had stopped reading. He was still staring at the "loves him" part and trying to decide if that was hyperbole or if she was telling the truth. Surely, she couldn't be in love with him after...

The service elevator rattled to a stop and Will stepped out. Then a vision walked in behind him, and Cash's heart became lodged in his throat.

Presley was wearing a black dress and high-heeled shoes. The very same, if memory served, as she'd worn when she'd shut herself into the elevator with him that past fated night.

"Look who I ran into in the lobby," Will said. "Small world. How far behind am I?"

"At least one," Luke said, pouring a whiskey for Will.

Cash stood from his seat, his brothers forgotten. She'd come back. To him.

She'd put her whole heart out there for him to see. He'd never had the guts to do that for her. He'd been too busy protecting himself. She said she'd set her world on fire for him. She said she'd have no regrets. Had she forgiven him after all?

"Hiya, cowboy," she said with a smile.

He reached her in a few long-legged steps and scooped her against him. Before he said a single word, he kissed her lips and hoped for the best.

He got it.

She wrapped her arms around his shoulders and wound her fingers in his hair and kissed him back. And damn, did that feel good. No, better than good. It felt *right*.

"Guessing you read my article?" she asked, her big blue eyes turned up to him.

"I love you, too."

Wetness clouded her eyes. "Cash."

"So much."

She grinned, and it lit up her entire face.

"Guessing you didn't win the contest," he said.

"Oh, I won."

"Yeah?"

"Yeah. I'm holding off booking my flight to London in case I'm needed in Tennessee."

"You're needed and not just in Tennessee." His turn to grin. "Just so happens my upcoming tour includes international stops."

"How convenient."

"I'm so sorry, Presley. For putting you through this not once, but twice. For not telling you how I feel about you. For not recognizing it at first, and then when I did, denying it. I had no idea the heavy feeling in my chest was you, crushing my heart into a million pieces."

She palmed his cheek. "You don't have to say anything else."

"I do. I should have told you the second I knew I was falling in love with you." He dropped his forehead to hers and murmured, "Which happened at the same moment you were falling in love with me. That rainy day on my couch."

He earned another longer, hotter, wetter kiss. It must have gone on a while. From the bar, he heard his brothers clear their throats and mutter under their breath.

When Presley's lips left Cash's, the only thing on his mind was taking her home. Taking off her dress. Taking his time once he had her underneath him.

"By the way, 'Lightning' is the song that needs to be rewritten."

"Beg your pardon?" He frowned.

"Well, see, you were wrong." She tightened her arms around his neck. "In our case, lightning struck twice."

"Does this mean I'm forgiven?"

"Yes."

His chest expanded.

"I'm not wasting another minute on regret or what-ifs."

"Aw, honey." He kissed her smile off her face, earning more mild protesting from his brothers. "You're my one in a million. Thanks for giving me another shot."

"Not so fast. You have some lost time to make up for," she whispered against his lips. "Let's get out of here."

"Good idea." He intertwined his fingers with hers and led her to the elevator, no need to steel himself for the ride down. After fearing the worst, that he'd lost her permanently, everything else that scared him was a joke. She loved him and he loved her and that was all he needed to feel ten feet tall and bulletproof.

"Hey!" Will called as Cash and Presley stepped onto the elevator. "What about the rewrite for 'Back for Good'?"

Cash glanced down at Presley, who squeezed his fingers and offered a gentle shake of her head. Then he looked up at his brothers and answered, "Think I'll leave it the way it is."

Epilogue

At the Cheshire, to a packed VIP crowd, Cash performed "Back for Good" for the first time in public.

In the front row stood Will and Hannah, Hallie, who had been peeking through her lashes at Gavin for most of the evening, and the love of Cash's life: Presley Cole.

Cash finished singing and Pres put her fingers between her lips and blew a loud whistle, the sound riling up the crowd.

"Hope you liked that one," he murmured into the microphone, letting his voice dip low. Pres loved it when he did that. She'd told him recently it sent shivers over her entire body. He'd personally checked every inch to be sure. "I have a bonus track to perform tonight. No one's ever heard it before. If that's okay with you all."

Predictably, the crowd cheered its approval.

He strummed his guitar and nodded to the band to go forth as they'd planned. Laughing, he returned to the mic and corrected. "I take it back. Presley Cole has heard a version of this song. I called it the 'Apology Song' but I've since changed a few lyrics. Pres, honey, you'll have to tell me if you like this one better."

She cocked her head, obviously curious. More whistles and cheers rose on the air, as Cash steeled himself and played the first few chords.

He cleared his throat and, eyes unwavering on his girl, he sang:

Dear Presley.
Will you marry me?
Make an honest man of me.
You mean everything.
Dear Presley.
I'll bring you coffee.
Every morning, gleefully.
Until you agree.
To marry me.
I hope you marry me.
You mean everything, Presley.

The crowd's cheers and whistles rose to ear-bleeding decibels, but he allowed them to fade into the background. There was only Presley, her gaze on him, her eyes welling with tears. She'd risked everything for him. He owed her the same.

"Irv," he said into the microphone. The beefy security guy cuffed Presley under the armpits and set her on the stage.

Demurely, she pushed her hair behind her ear and bit her lip. Cash, his grin unstoppable, turned his guitar facedown and gave it a good shake. He caught the diamond ring in his hand before it hit the stage.

She covered her mouth with her palms before shakily offering her left hand. The crowd roared their approval. He heard his brothers over all of them, shouting their encouragement the loudest. Cash slid the ring onto Presley's finger and then she hugged him so tight he had to fight for his next breath.

Viral Pop would beg her for weeks to disclose what she'd whispered into his ear at that moment, but she refused to confess.

She and Cash would argue for years about whether readers would be disappointed if they knew what she'd said, or if not knowing made the story better. In the end they decided it didn't matter.

Cash and Presley had each other, and there was nowhere he'd rather be than in her arms. Whether on the dock writing songs, on the couch making love while it rained, or on his boat, floating under the starry, nighttime sky.

He'd found his forever.

Twice, as it'd turned out.

* * * * *

*Look for the next Dynasties: Beaumont Bay novel,
coming next month from* USA TODAY
bestselling author Jules Bennett!

Fake Engagement, Nashville Style

#2809 TEXAS TOUGH
Texas Cattleman's Club: Heir Apparent • by Janice Maynard
World-traveling documentary filmmaker Abby Carmichael is only in Royal for a short project, definitely not to fall for hometown rancher Carter Crane. But opposites attract and the sparks between them ignite! Can they look past their differences for something more than temporary?

#2810 ONE WEEK TO CLAIM IT ALL
Sambrano Studios • by Adriana Herrera
The illegitimate daughter of a telenovela mogul, Esmeralda Sambrano is shocked to learn *she's* the successor to his empire, much to the chagrin of her father's protégé, Rodrigo Almanzar. Tension soon turns to passion, but will a common enemy ruin everything?

#2811 FAKE ENGAGEMENT, NASHVILLE STYLE
Dynasties: Beaumont Bay • by Jules Bennett
Tired of being Nashville's most eligible bachelor, Luke Sutherland needs a fake date to the wedding of the year, and his ex lover, Cassandra Taylor, needs a favor. But as they masquerade as a couple, one hot kiss makes things all too real...

#2812 A NINE-MONTH TEMPTATION
Brooklyn Nights • by Joanne Rock
Sable Cordero's dream job as a celebrity stylist is upended after she spends one sexy night with fashion CEO Roman Zayn. When he learns Sable is pregnant, he promises to take care of his child, nothing more. But neither anticipated the attraction still between them...

#2813 WHAT HAPPENS IN MIAMI...
Miami Famous • by Nadine Gonzalez
Actor Alessandro Cardenas isn't just attending Miami's hottest art event for the parties. He's looking to find who forged his grandfather's famous paintings. When he meets gallerist Angeline Louis, he can't resist at least one night...but will that lead to betrayal?

#2814 CORNER OFFICE SECRETS
Men of Maddox Hill • by Shannon McKenna
Chief finance officer Vann Acosta is not one to mix business with pleasure—until he meets stunning cybersecurity expert Sophie Valente. Their chemistry is undeniable, but when she uncovers the truth, will company secrets change everything?

HDCNM0621

*The illegitimate daughter of a telenovela mogul,
Esmeralda Sambrano-Peña is shocked to learn she's
the successor to his empire, much to the chagrin of her
father's protégé, Rodrigo Almanzar. Tension soon turns
to passion, but will a common enemy ruin everything?*

Read on for a sneak peek at
One Week to Claim It All
by Adriana Herrera.

"I want to kiss you, Esmeralda."

She shook her head at the statement, even as a
frustrated little whine escaped her lips. Her arms were
already circling around his neck. "If we're going to do
this, just do it, Rodrigo."

Without hesitation he crushed his mouth into hers and
the world fell away. This man could be harbor in any
storm, always had been. His tongue stole into her mouth,
and it was like not a single day had passed since they'd
last done this.

She pressed herself to him as he peppered her neck
with fluttering kisses. Somewhere in the back of her mind
she knew this was the height of stupidity, that they were
both being reckless. That if anyone found out about this,
she would probably sink her chances of getting approved

by the board. But it was so hard to think when he was whispering intoxicatingly delicious things in Spanish. *Preciosa, amada… Mia.*

It was madness for him to call her his, and what was worse, she reveled in it. She wanted it so desperately that her skin prickled, her body tightening and loosening in places under his skilled touch.

"I can't get enough of you. I never was able to." He sounded bewildered. Like he couldn't quite figure out how it was that he'd gotten there.

Welcome to the club.

Esmeralda knew they should stop. They were supposed to head to the party soon and she'd for sure have to refresh her makeup now that she'd decided to throw all her boundaries out the window. But instead of stopping, she threw her head back and let him make his way down her neck, his teeth grazing her skin as he tightened one hand on her butt and the other pulled down the strap of her dress.

"Can I kiss you here?" he asked as his breath feathered over her breasts.

"Yes." She was on an express bus to Bad Decision Central and she could not be bothered to stop.

Don't miss what happens next in…
One Week to Claim It All
by Adriana Herrera,
the first book in her new Sambrano Studios series!

Available soon wherever
Harlequin Desire books and ebooks are sold.

Harlequin.com

Get 4 FREE REWARDS!

We'll send you 2 FREE Books plus 2 FREE Mystery Gifts.

Harlequin Desire books transport you to the world of the American elite with juicy plot twists, delicious sensuality and intriguing scandal.

FREE Value Over $20

YES! Please send me 2 FREE Harlequin Desire novels and my 2 FREE gifts (gifts are worth about $10 retail). After receiving them, if I don't wish to receive any more books, I can return the shipping statement marked "cancel." If I don't cancel, I will receive 6 brand-new novels every month and be billed just $4.55 per book in the U.S. or $5.24 per book in Canada. That's a savings of at least 13% off the cover price! It's quite a bargain! Shipping and handling is just 50¢ per book in the U.S. and $1.25 per book in Canada.* I understand that accepting the 2 free books and gifts places me under no obligation to buy anything. I can always return a shipment and cancel at any time. The free books and gifts are mine to keep no matter what I decide.

225/326 HDN GNND

Name (please print)

Address   Apt. #

City   State/Province   Zip/Postal Code

Email: Please check this box ☐ if you would like to receive newsletters and promotional emails from Harlequin Enterprises ULC and its affiliates. You can unsubscribe anytime.

Mail to the **Harlequin Reader Service:**
IN U.S.A.: P.O. Box 1341, Buffalo, NY 14240-8531
IN CANADA: P.O. Box 603, Fort Erie, Ontario L2A 5X3

Want to try 2 free books from another series! Call 1-800-873-8635 or visit www.ReaderService.com.

*Terms and prices subject to change without notice. Prices do not include sales taxes, which will be charged (if applicable) based on your state or country of residence. Canadian residents will be charged applicable taxes. Offer not valid in Quebec. This offer is limited to one order per household. Books received may not be as shown. Not valid for current subscribers to Harlequin Desire books. All orders subject to approval. Credit or debit balances in a customer's account(s) may be offset by any other outstanding balance owed by or to the customer. Please allow 4 to 6 weeks for delivery. Offer available while quantities last.

Your Privacy—Your information is being collected by Harlequin Enterprises ULC, operating as Harlequin Reader Service. For a complete summary of the information we collect, how we use this information and to whom it is disclosed, please visit our privacy notice located at corporate.harlequin.com/privacy-notice. From time to time we may also exchange your personal information with reputable third parties. If you wish to opt out of this sharing of your personal information, please visit readerservice.com/consumerschoice or call 1-800-873-8635. **Notice to California Residents**—Under California law, you have specific rights to control and access your data. For more information on these rights and how to exercise them, visit corporate.harlequin.com/california-privacy.

HD21R